CITRON
PRESS

RONALD **BARNES**

Ronald Barnes was born in Edinburgh and started out as an actor playing in weekly rep, musicals and cabaret. One of his plays was bought for Broadway, and performed on BBC Radio. He worked for Pan American Airways in Reservations Control before moving to Milan, where he taught English at Bergamo University and the British Council. He eventually founded his own school - English for Italians. His textbooks have been published in Italy and the UK.

On returning to England, he settled in Deal, Kent, where he teaches Italian for GCSE and Adult Learners.

This is his third novel.

For Dennis Wood

CITRON PRESS

Fresh ideas from

NEW AUTHORS
CO-OPERATIVE

Published by Citron Press
Connors Corp. Ltd., Suite 155 Business Design Centre,
52 Upper Street, Islington Green, London N1 0QH, Great Britain
www.citronpress.co.uk

ISBN 0754400166

Printed and bound in Great Britain by Esparto Digital Ltd., Slack Lane, Derby.

A copy of this book is held at the British Library.

●**THE KASHMIR** BLUE

RONALD **BARNES**●

WANTED: Strong, tough guy to look after old, but rich homosexual. Foreign travel envisaged. Full details and photo to Box 973 Kent Advertiser

Well, that looked a right pushover, didn't it? I thought - get in with the old poofter, take what's going and scarper with the proceeds. But it didn't happen like that. In fact, I'd never have guessed what would happen.

So I wrote a few lines about meself. The usual come-on stuff: six foot tall, early thirties, broad-shouldered, strong and healthy. Enclosed a photo Maggie took of me lying in bed after we'd had the most fantastic – anyway, it looked real good in colour – and sent it off.

I didn't tell Maggie, though. Dunno why. Anyway, it's true I'm six foot tall – well, five ten, and well built in every department. I exercise once a week in the gym. I don't drink much neither. But early thirties is going it a bit. More thirty-five-ish, but I still look good. Hair's dark brown and cut short, and right now I'm ready for anything.

CHAPTER ONE

The reply came by return. Well, a week later. Very short and to the point. Would I care to meet the gentleman at the County Hotel in Dover at 11.30 Wednesday next? My travel expenses would be refunded, and twenty quid in my thick hand for my trouble. Elegant, arty signature: Richard Grayson. Phone my reply.

I rang straight away, but got the answerphone. I hung up and tried again later. I wanted to hear what the old boy sounded like. But in the end I had to leave a message. I felt excited like, but still I said nothing to Maggie. I didn't really think she'd need to know until the foreign travel came up. And if that was a weekend in Amsterdam, he could forget it.

The week passed slowly as usual: nothing much happened – at least, nothing good. I'm smoking too much. What the hell. I'm not going nowhere, everything's a mess. I'm losing it, I thought to meself, I'm losing it. This is bloody middle age.

Maggie was working overtime that week – she's at Sainsbury's, and looking for promotion – so I had a lot of time to meself. It's been a good relationship: we've been together for over a year now and set ourselves up quite nicely in this flat in Ashford, even if it is a bit small. She'd had a rough time like before I met her: she'd been married to some git called Ian, and come down south from Edinburgh to get over him. She's a real belter with lovely long red hair and that pale skin that goes with it like, which is more than I can say for her ugly sister, Janet – a right fishwife that one.

But I hardly see Maggie these days. She comes home from work tired and tetchy. Not my fault she has to work so hard. She wants to. At least she says she does. Bloody lucky to be in work. There's nothing for me out there. Not that I'm much good at anything, really. Kind of odd-job man, I suppose. I'm good at mending things, and can do a bit of painting and that. Nothing expert.

But there you go.

RICHARD

I took to Steve the moment he walked into the room. He's tallish and well built, without that over-developed muscular look. He's not handsome: sexy, yes, but not handsome. He grinned at me, and held out his hand. His grasp was strong and pleasurable.

'Hi,' he said. 'I'm Steve Jackman.'

He talked about himself openly, but I wondered if he was telling me the whole truth. Only when I asked him if he had ever been in prison did he hesitate for a moment. Not that I care. I explained that whatever he was or whatever he had done, I wanted someone who would always be honest with me.

He seemed taken aback.

'Have you a problem with that?' I asked.

'Nah. Nah, it's just – '

'What?'

'Unusual, innit?' I was to find out that whenever he became apprehensive, he lapsed into the demotic.

'The whole situation is unusual though, isn't it?'

'What is it then. The situation? Like?' he muttered, a bit ruffled. He started to fidget, and I took pleasure in that. I enjoyed being in control.

'I've got others to see,' I said finally. 'We'll be in touch.'

He was discomfited at this. 'You mean nothin's settled yet?'

'Absolutely nothing. I've got some decisions to make.'

He looked disappointed, which I found endearing. But he got up and turned to go.

'I'll phone you,' I said.

'Nah,' he replied quickly. 'Don't do that. Can't I phone you?'

'Absolutely not,' I said.

He hesitated. 'I still dunno what this is about. Whad'ya want from me?'

'Exactly what the advertisement said. I want, or need, a strong tough man to help me.'

'Do what?'

'I'll explain later.'

'Why not now?'

'Let's just say I prefer to leave it till later.'

He nodded noncommittally, then grinned. 'What's the bit about foreign travel then?'

It certainly was a likeable grin.

'Samoa,' I said.

He sat down again. 'Samoa?'

I had a feeling he didn't know where it was, but would look up a map as soon as he left the room.

'Yes. But other places as well. You have a valid passport?'

He nodded.

'Good. I'll ring you when I've come to a decision.'

He nodded again. And went to the door. Fully recovered, he turned and gave me that great grin.

'Cheers,' he said.

And left.

STEVE

You could have knocked me down with the proverbial. Samoa. Where the hell's that? South Pacific, innit? Then other places, he said. Blimey, he must be rich. He's in quite good nick, though, except for his weight. Enjoys life and his food, that's obvious. Looks well over seventy to me. Thick white hair too, but black eyebrows. Weird that. Don't think they're dyed neither. It's what you might call a strong face but gone a bit puffy – with the booze I shouldn't wonder. And then there's his eyes, very off-putting they are. They stare straight into you. Amazing blue colour. I thought eyes faded when you got older, but his haven't. They're real piercing, like.

Still, I can't make him out. What does he want with me? He looks healthy enough, so he don't need a nurse. Is he so rich he needs a minder? If so, then why not say so, straight out? That only leaves one other alternative. He wants me in bed. Well, sex with a guy's not for me. God, what a stupid fool I am. If Maggie finds out what I'm up to, she'll crucify me. I'd better ring the old boy at once and tell him no go. Whatever it is.

Still. I wouldn't mind Samoa. Dusky maidens and all that. Perhaps I could swing it somehow. Anyway, let's wait and see. Probably he'll find someone more willing.

I wonder how much he's paying? He never said, come to think of it.

RICHARD

I've almost decided on Steve. There may be something disingenuous about him, yet I think we'll get on once various things are sorted out. The response to my ad had been less enthusiastic than I had hoped. Most of them went straight into the basket. It's extraordinary what the word 'rich' does to people: I put it in the ad, thinking it would attract a certain type, forgetting that 'rich' attracts all types. I suppose it was to be expected that they would all imagine it was a sex ad, because they all said or implied that they had a price.

Except Steve. He didn't mention the word sex, or price. He gets brownie points for that. He's clearly not well educated, although he tries to speak 'proper' as he would say. He told me both his parents died when he was young, and that he and his brother were brought up by his aunt in Penrith. He left when he was twenty and came down to London on his own to seek his fortune. Like most he ended up fighting for his existence, but eventually he got a job with a construction firm. He seems to have drifted through life having one affair after another, with no long-term commitment until he was on a job in Ashford, when he met this girl, Maggie, and moved in with her. His accent has a few northern vowels, but most of his grammar is Estuary English.

In the end I interviewed only six men of different shapes and sizes. What liars we all are. Some put their ages too low, some too high. Most emphasised their physical attributes and overstated them into the bargain. They all gave me the glad eye, and they all lied one way or another.

Steve didn't. At least not directly, though he is hiding something. But I don't think it's serious. He's a fascinating character with a cheerful disposition – very important for me. He is one of those people who can look you in the eye and make you feel you're the only one they want to be with. Not true of course, but he makes me feel good.

It's really down to three. Steve, Mike and Don. They're all about the same age, and they all look reasonably attractive. Only Don is the real tough guy, with tattoos all over his brown arms. He's the one who works out in the local gym every day. He's really strong and tough. But not much on top, I should imagine.

Mike is dark, hairy and foreign looking. Very handsome. Small and wiry. Difficult to imagine how strong he is, but he's no weakling. A plumber he told me. At least he's got a trade.

But Steve – he doesn't seem to have a trade or a job, but he gives a very positive first impression: his hazel eyes look straight at you. His dark brown hair has flecks of gold in it – I'm not sure whether these are artificial or natural. It's cut very short, with a few strands falling on his brow. His largish ears stick out rather, so that when he leans back in his chair, hands behind his head, he has a look of Puck with that impish grin. But his boyish smile belies his years: the lines round his eyes place him well in his thirties. At the same time, he can look quite tough with his tattoo and earring in his left ear. The earring and tattoo seem mandatory to macho men these days, but not all of them can carry it off. Steve can. Like Don, he's got a tattoo on his arm, but somehow this adds to his sexiness. I've got to admit it: Steve is very sexy. He could make me feel out of control: you're not supposed to be affected by sex when you're old; you're supposed to sublimate it – but age never wearies that part of you, although society will condemn. And that's what worries me about Steve: I might not be able to stay in control. Once he realises he could twist me round his strong fingers, I would be in his power, and not the other way around.

He's what the Italians call *nervoso*. That is, he's not exactly jumpy, but there is nothing still about him. He's restless and on edge all the time. There's a lot of energy inside that man if one could find the right way to unleash it. And maybe that's what I'm afraid of.

I've arranged to see all three of them again in two days' time. But I've pretty well decided already.

MAGGIE

I don't know what's got into Steve these days, but he's gone all quiet and broody. The great thing about Steve is his cheerful smile and attitude to life; but he's not the same at all. I wonder if he's having an affair. There was that besom in the pub two weeks ago he seemed keen on, but I don't think he followed it up. You never know though.

But yesterday evening when I came home from a late shift, he was lying on the bed staring at the ceiling, and didn't even say hello. I asked him what was wrong, but he just stubbed out his cigarette, and turned over. Usually he gets up and makes me a cup of tea or pours me a drink, but he just lay there sulking. Though what about, God knows.

I had a shower, but still felt tense and irritable. When I came out of the bathroom, he was still lying on the bed. 'Come here, Maggie,' he said. His voice was husky, and normally I would have laughed. I thought he was joking, playing games or something. But something in his face made me stop laughing.

This wasn't the moment, and I said so.

He grabbed me roughly by the arm and pulled me down to him. I tried to resist, but he's too strong for me. He's never been like that before. Normally he's forceful, and a bit rough perhaps, but gentle with it too. He's a good wee soul really, and I must admit part of his attraction is his ability to be rough and gentle at the same time. But that time I felt powerless. The next morning before I could say what I felt, he got up, lit another cigarette and went out of the flat, slamming the door behind him.

Not like him at all.

STEVE

Maggie smells a rat, I think. She's gone all funny with me. We're hardly speaking. It's not my fault, is it? I've done nothing wrong. At least not yet.

This morning at breakfast, she glowered at me. 'What's wrong, Steve?' she said finally.

'Whad'ya mean – what's wrong?'

'You know perfectly well what I mean.'

The usual exchanges people make. Better to make a tape of them, then we wouldn't need to speak at all.

'You've changed recently,' she said. God, the tape was continuing. 'You've lost your sparkle.'

Yeah, that was possible. I don't feel at all happy since I met that bloody poofter, and was feeling even worse this morning as he had called me back for 'the final interview' as he called it, and I wanted to get out of the flat.

'And what are you all dressed up for?' she was eyeing the snazzy tie I'd just bought.

What can I say? I really like Maggie, you know. She's a great girl. She's got great red hair, real silky as the commercials say, and legs that go on forever. She's always there for me, but I dunno.

'Like it?' I asked. 'Cost six quid in the market.'

'Looks it too.' She loves to put me down. 'Why did you buy a tie? You hate ties.'

'Got a job interview,' I mumbled.

'What?' she cried. 'You? You've got a job interview?

'What's so strange about that? Ain't ya pleased for me?'

She softened at once. 'Course I am,' she smiled, and put her arms round me. She plonked a nice wet one on my mouth.

'Here,' I cried playfully, 'don't get me all worked up now, will ya?'

'What's it for?'

'What?'

'The job, of course. What's it for?'

'Oh,' I said. 'Some old geezer wants an odd-job man.'

Those great green eyes of hers looked at me. 'What do you need a tie for? Odd jobs don't need ties.'

'I just want to make a good impression,' I said feebly.

'Well, you won't with that tie. It's common.'

I got out of the house as quick as I could. I must tell her something. But what? I'll wait until this interview is over, then I can really talk to her.

You might have known it would be pissing with rain when I got out of the train at Dover station. It was late as well, so I wasn't in the best of moods, was I, when I ran into the County Hotel, soaked to the skin.

A right royal mess I looked, I can tell you.

They sent me up to the same room as before, and I squelched out of the lift with a confidence rate of zero. I wasn't too pleased to see this guy coming down the corridor towards me neither. He looked like a contender, and a good one at that. Bare arms, all tattooed, hair well greased down. six foot and aggressive. I wasn't expecting competition.

Anyway, I straightened the tie, checked my flies and knocked.

'Enter,' said the voice. Sounded very grand.

One final check on me flies, and in I went.

He was writing at one of those stupid little desks they have in hotels. Not that I've been in many in this country. Most hotels I know have been in the 'costa Brava and Tenerife.

He looked up. 'Ah, Mr Jackman,' he said. 'Sit down, will you? I shan't keep you a minute.'

What a cheek. I looked round for a chair, but there was only this small thing facing the window. The rain had stopped and the sun was shining straight into my face. I suppose he arranged that too. Typical English weather; I was wet and looked a mess. Well, it wouldn't be long before I was out of here and heading back home.

He stopped writing, turned and looked at me as if he hadn't seen me before.

'Well now,' he said in that posh voice of his. 'Have you thought over what we talked about at our last meeting?

What's he on about? We didn't talk about nothing far as I remember. No particulars that's for sure. So I just shrugged.

He looked at me irritated. 'Mr Jackman,' he said. 'I asked you a question.'

'I don't understand it,' I said giving him a grin.

'Are you interested in my project or not?'

'Might be, if I knew what it was.'

He sighed. 'You're not being very helpful, Mr Jackman,' he said.

'Only because I dunno what you're talking about.'

Another sigh. This wasn't going at all well. He was staring at me as if he'd never seen me before, so I stared back. I was getting right pissed off.

He opened his mouth to say something, then changed his mind. He fiddled with his pen and doodled on the paper on the desk. Then he looked at me again, and his face softened. In fact, he looked defenceless. I felt sorry for him like.

'What's up, mate?' I enquired. The mate bit slipped out, and I thought he would take offence.

But he smiled and said: 'Just thinking.' He fiddled with his papers. 'Tell me about yourself, Mr Jackman,' he said.

We'd been through all this the last time. I couldn't quite remember what I'd said. I didn't want to be caught telling porkies.

'Whad'ya wanna know?' I asked.

'How old are you?'

'I told ya, 35.'

He squinted at me. 'Are you married?'

'I told ya, no.'

'Have you any commitments?

'Whad'ya mean?'

'Is there anyone serious in your life?'

It was none of his business. But I couldn't say that, could I? Anyway, I could see what he was getting at. 'Nothing that need concern you,' I replied loftily.

He smiled at that. 'You told me you had a girlfriend.'

'So?'

'As long as I know. What will she say about you going on these trips with me?'

What the hell was I supposed to reply to that one? 'I've still got to discuss the details with her,' I replied. 'That is, when I know the details meself.'

He seemed satisfied with that. 'Fair enough. Have you ever been in prison?' He changed tack abruptly.

'You asked me that before.'

'And you didn't reply. You changed the subject.'

What was I to say to that? Last time, he'd gone on about being honest and that. So I'll tell him. 'Not exactly,' I said. 'But I was had up for assault.'

'You're violent then?' he asked.

'Nah – just don't like being insulted, that's all.'

'Tell me about it,' he said.

'Me mate Jock and me was having a bevvy in the local, quiet like, when this geezer started in on us. This was like ten, eleven years ago. Said he'd seen Jock's missus with some guy at Jock's plant. Called her a slag. Well – not exactly – but pretty near. Implied it like. Jock took offence, and went for him. And I backed him up like.'

'And they sent you down for that?'

'Well, not exactly. We was booked in custody overnight, and cautioned the next day like. But we was in the pub the following week, Cynthia and me. That was me girlfriend at the time. And this same geezer comes over to her and chats her up like, while I'm outside having a slash. I told him to piss off, and he started to get nasty. One thing led to another, and before you know it I'd given him one. And that started like what they called an assault. I was bound over and that, then hauled up in front of the magistrate. It was my lucky day, 'cos he didn't put me away but fined me hundred quid.'

He nodded, satisfied. 'But your current girlfriend's called Maggie, isn't she?'

'Yeah. Cynthia was ten years ago.'

'This Maggie. Is your relationship serious?'

'Sort of,' I hedged.

'You don't seem very sure.'

'Well,' I still hedged. I didn't know what he wanted me to say. 'Depends,' I answered finally.

'On what?'

'On what's happening here, ' I said.

The sun had gone in again, and rain was spitting on the window. God, what a country. It was June, after all. Me feet were wet, and I was hungry. Could do with a fag, too.

He was fiddling at the desk again and a silence grew between us, like the grey mist outside. I couldn't stand much more of this. 'So what's the big deal?' I burst out.

'Deal?' He looked bemused.

'Yeah. What's the situation?'

'Oh,' he said, 'You've got a valid passport, haven't you?'

'Yeah,' I said. 'I told you last time.'

'So you did.' He fiddled some more. Suddenly he made his mind up. 'Right,' he said. 'The deal is this. You are to accompany me on my trips abroad, look after me, and protect me.'

'Protect you?' I said alarmed. 'What from?'

'You never know. Nothing in particular. Just in case.'

'In case of what?' Something wasn't quite right here.

'Look,' he was getting annoyed. 'Do you want this job or not?'

'I'm not very clear about – '

'Everything is perfectly clear.' He tapped his fingers on the desk. 'Either you accept the job or you don't. Which is it to be?'

I was desperate for a fag. 'It's a bit vague,' I muttered.

'What's vague about it?'

'Well,' I answered. 'There's no detail. When does this start? Is this a 24-hour job, or do I get home at night? What are we going for? Are these holidays, or what? And,' I added, at last asking the most important question, 'how much are you paying?'

He smiled at that, and the tension was broken between us. Funny that, but when he smiled, those piercing eyes of his changed to a merry twinkle. He looked real kind when his face softened, so I grinned back.

'It starts next week when we fly to Morocco - '

'Morocco?' I interrupted. 'Thought you said Samoa.'

'Samoa comes later. It's a twenty-four hour job, as you put it, while we're away. When we're in England, you can stay at home. With Maggie, I presume.'

There was a slight touch of acid in that last bit.

'And the money?' I prompted.

'A hundred pounds a day while abroad. And £50 retainer a day at home.'

I gasped, but not too loud. Even I can add that up. Minimum, a pony a day was £350 a week for doing nothing. The rest would add up to a pile of dosh no time at all. Mustn't look too eager.

'Well?' he asked.

I was just about to accept as grandly as I could, when it struck me that this was an awful lot of money for very little in the way of work. Was sex part of the deal?

'What's the catch?' I said.

'Catch?' he stared haughtily. 'There's no catch.'

'It looks a lot of dough for not much.'

He smiled. 'If you prefer to take less, I would be perfectly willing to – '

'No, no I don't mean that,' I said hastily. 'But is that all I have to do? Just go with you abroad?'

He nodded. 'That's all.'

I had to get this out of the way. 'Er – do we have separate rooms?' I thought I'd phrased that rather well.

He stared at me. 'Of course,' he said, all hoity-toity. 'I never share rooms with anyone. Why should I?'

That was a relief. If he comes knocking at the door in the middle of the night, I can soon put him off.

'That's all right then. You're on.'

'By that I presume you mean you accept?'

'Too right,' I said.

'Good. I'll phone you next week with the flight details. Oh, and just pack a few things. We won't be staying long in Morocco. And we'll be coming back home before our next jaunt.'

That was that then. All I had to do was square it with Maggie.

MAGGIE

I knew there was something up the moment he came in the door. He was wet and bedraggled, cursing at the weather, but I could see from his face that this was an excuse. Something was up.

I went on with the cooking. He didn't speak but went straight into the bedroom. No greeting, nothing. I turned the gas down low and followed him in. 'And hello to you too,' I said.

'I'm soaked through.' He was tearing off his clothes.

'Where have you been to get so wet then?' I asked.

'Tell you later, once I get meself dry.'

'No,' I said firmly. 'Tell me now.' You have to be firm with him, or else he wriggles out of things.

He was upset and angry. It was serious this time. I decided to bide my whisht. 'Want a coffee?'

'That'd be good,' he said, still not looking at me.

I went back to the kitchen and put the kettle on. After a while he came in.

'So?' I prompted.

'So,' he said. I gave him his coffee and stood waiting.

'You won't believe this,' he said with an attempt at a grin. 'I've got me a job.'

That was a relief. He wasn't in trouble with the cops then.

'That's great,' I cried, and put my arms round him.

'It means travelling though,' he said. 'Abroad.'

'You? Travelling abroad.?' I didn't mean to sound incredulous. Not that he's stupid or anything. Actually he can be very bright sometimes, in spite of his sketchy education.

'Yeah. That surprises you, don't it? 'Again the wry grin.

'Where? What for? Tell me everything.'

'Well it's this geezer like,' he said. 'He's offered me this job, like. Travelling abroad with him, to foreign parts, like. To look after him.'

'Look after him?' I repeated. 'Why? Is he ill?'

'Nah. Just old, and a bit lonely.'

Sounded fishy to me, and I said so.

He squirmed in his chair and lit a cigarette. 'Not fishy at all,' he inhaled and blew silly smoke rings.

'What's his job then? What does he do?'

'Job?' he said. 'Dunno. Didn't ask.'

'Whyever not? What do you have to do?'

'I told ya. Look after him. He's old, and that. He's retired.'

'But why you? What does he need a nurse for? And if not a nurse, then a bodyguard? And you're neither.'

'Look, what's all this questioning? I'm going to Morocco next week. And then Samoa.'

'Samoa?' I sat down at that. What kind of job could he have got himself into? There's none so queer as folk, and none so daft as Steve when it comes to money. 'How much is he paying you?' I asked. 'Presumably, he's paying you something for all this?'

'Course he is. Quite a lot, actually.'

'How much?' I persevered.

'Never mind.' He gulped down his coffee and got up. 'Tell you what. We'll go out to celebrate. Take you to that new bistro, or whatever they call it. You can practise your French then, can't yer?'

'Steve -' I began.

'Can't stop now,' he broke in. 'Got things to do. See you later.' And rushed out of the flat.

I couldn't take it all in. His attitude was wrong, the job was wrong, or looked that way. Who was this man? And what was it all about?

But I never did find out. At least not the whole story. Steve just wouldn't talk to me about it. But it changed our relationship in some way, and I couldn't put my finger on it. It was so stupid: he'd got a job, hadn't he? Why couldn't I be supportive, cheer him on so to speak, instead of being suspicious? I hadn't even met the man, so what did I know?

He's a funny mixture is Steve: he's very cheerful and full of life, but there's something that makes him restive, and I don't know how to deal with it. He doesn't like talking about his past and it's all very vague, but I gather he had a long-term relationship with a woman called Cynthia. She got pregnant, but had a miscarriage. They split up soon after that, and he drifted from one job to another, never settling down till he met me.

The night before Steve left, he took me out to dinner at that really posh place in the High Street – can't remember the name. We sat in the candlelight, and he looked so sweet and loveable. I could kill him the way he can affect me like that. I'll never learn. I wanted to ask him more about the job, yet I didn't want to break the mood.

We had a great meal, went home pleasantly placed, as we say in Edinburgh. Steve made love to me that night – really made love to me, not that rough rape of a week ago. His tongue was everywhere, he groaned and whimpered.

I was his girl again, like old times. We slept in each other's arms.

Next morning he got up without a word, avoided my eye, and left with his case crammed any old how. He hadn't wanted me to help him pack. He just went. I sat down and cried.

CHAPTER TWO

Richard

Steve Jackman looked an absolute wreck when I picked him up in the hire car. We drove to Heathrow in silence; I didn't like the mood he was in, and was beginning to regret my choice. At least the trip to Morocco would be short, and I could abort the whole thing fairly quickly if necessary. I tried to break the silence.

'Got your passport?' I asked.

'Course,' was his succinct reply.

So he's moody. But why? There must be trouble at home with his girlfriend, but I didn't like to ask.

'Been to Morocco before?'

'Nah. You know I haven't. Told you the first time.'

'Look.' I was getting exasperated. 'I don't know what your problem is, and why you're in this childish mood. But whatever it is, snap out of it. Please remember that you are at this moment on duty, so to speak. I don't expect you to be full of jokes all the time, but neither do I want the company of a spoilt child. Either you pull yourself together, or you turn round and go home.'

He didn't answer for a while, and I was on the point of stopping the car (though what we could have done halfway up the M20 I hadn't quite worked out) when he grunted.

'What was that?'

'Right,' he mumbled.

'What do you mean – right?'

'You're right.' He had the grace to look sheepish. 'It's just I'm a bit nervous, I suppose.'

'Of what?'

'The whole thing. The whole business. I dunno what I'm supposed to be doing like. '

'I thought I had explained to you most carefully.'

'Well, you haven't. I dunno if I'm supposed to be your nurse or your bodyguard or what.'

'Oh,' I said relieved. 'Is that all? A bit of both I suppose.'

'Yeh well. I'm not neither, am I? I'm not a trained nurse, and I ain't no gorilla.'

'You can be both as far as I'm concerned. I chose you, remember, so I think you're right for me. '

He relaxed somewhat after that. He didn't say much more, but the rest of the journey was less tense.

STEVE

All the way to the airport I was thinking of Maggie and how I'd left her like that. I can be a shit sometimes, I know. But I dunno. What could I say? She disapproved of the whole thing that was clear, and I'm not sure what I'm doing with this old geezer. It was getting right sinister, like. He didn't say a word, not even welcome or nothing, and we just sat there, side by side in this car he'd hired. I was like on the point of saying it was no go when he suddenly asked if I'd got my passport. Stupid git.

He then got stroppy with me and told me to stop sulking as if I was a child. I could've planted one on that pudgy nose of his, but instead I got stroppy too and asked him what it was all about. He calmed down after that, and we didn't speak again till we got to check-in.

MAGGIE

Not a word from Steve. I thought he might ring me, but I suppose he was too busy at the airport buying his duty-frees and stuff. I don't know. Our relationship doesn't look good. What is he up to? He's being so cagey about all this, and I just don't believe a word of it.

To cap it all, I've got to work extra shifts and I'm absolutely knackered. My sister, Janet, says it's good I'm so busy, and it's better not to dwell on things too much. It'll all come out right in the end, she says. Why do people always say it'll be all right in the end, when it's perfectly obvious that it won't?

I got home at lunch time: thought of him sunning himself in Morocco, and thought what am I doing with a bloke who can't even trust me enough to tell me what's going on? If he doesn't phone me tomorrow, then we're on our way to a serious discussion. We've got to get this sorted.

STEVE

Well, I don't think much of Morocco. They never stop hassling you. Selling this, selling that, they follow you everywhere. I could give them a smack in the eye all right. His nibs don't seem bothered. He sails ahead like royalty, while I follow a foot behind shouting 'piss off' to all and sundry.

Anyway, we're shacked up in this nice hostelry called El Minzah. Must say the hotel's a bit of all right, once you've got through the grotty entrance. There's a nice pool, and satellite telly in the bedroom. No problem with the sleeping arrangements, I must say. He went straight to his room the moment we arrived and didn't emerge till next morning. I got a crisp phone call from his room that evening to go out and enjoy myself like. He was going to bed early and eating in his room. So out I went into the sinful streets of Tangier. Apart from being packed with people, all moving the opposite way from me, I couldn't see much sin about. Tell the truth, I didn't feel like going too far from the hotel – my sense of direction isn't too hot – and I didn't fancy losing my way amongst all these jabbering foreigners.

What I'm doing here I don't know. Seem to be saying that a lot these days, but it all seems too good to be true. Anyway, next day, I have me breakfast in a kind of courtyard like – quite good it was too, with a fountain playing and all – and then take myself to the pool for a nice bit of suntan. Out comes his nibs in as bad a temper as I've ever seen him in.

'Where have you been?' he spits.

'Here. Like you told me,' I reply, calm as you like. 'Had a bit of brekkie, then onto the sunbed. Whad'ya expect?'

'You're supposed to be watching over me,' he snivels.

'Well, can't do that, can I, if I dunno what you're up to and that.' I felt pleased with that remark. Sticking up for meself and all. Showed him I won't be pushed around.

'For God's sake get out of that ridiculous outfit and come with me,' he rapped.

'Where are we going then?'

'Down to the port. Keep close to me too. I'm carrying a lot of money with me.'

It wasn't till later I wondered what the hell he was doing waltzing through those alleys with a load of dosh in his pocket. But that's Dickie for ya.

RICHARD

This young man is turning out to be very bad news indeed. I let him have the evening off, and instead of reporting fresh and keen the next morning, I have to trawl the hotel to find him. There he was, sprawled out on a sunbed with a silly little hat on this head and very little else, grinning from ear to ear. I gave him a good ticking off, and when I told him to get dressed at once, instead of looking contrite, he behaved as if nothing was wrong and sauntered back to his room to change. He finally appeared in bright shorts and the ubiquitous T-shirt and gave me a mock salute.

Getting very saucy indeed.

When I told him to stay close to me, he gave me a knowing grin and asked if I wanted to take his arm. He is a definite mistake. The sooner we get back to England and I drop him the better.

STEVE

Well that was what I'd call an adventure worthy of Schwarzenegger or whatever he's called.

We was going down to the port, down this grotty street, more like an alley than a proper street; I was keeping close to him like he said, though we weren't touching or anything like that. We was passing a lot of shops, at least they would call them shops, but they weren't no Sainsburys I can tell you. As I said, we was walking down quite fast, minding our own business when suddenly his nibs stops and says:

'That's the place.'

'What place?' I ask. But before I could say the proverbial Jack Robinson, he'd scuttled into this dark looking clothes shop full of them long dresses Arabs wear. I followed him in, not liking this one bit, and saw him talking to this old geezer with very few teeth and a dirty what-d'ya-call-it on. His nibs caught sight of me.

'Wait outside,' he cried. 'Shan't be long.'

'I thought I was supposed to stay beside you all the time.'

'Quite right,' he cried. 'You've done splendidly. Just go outside for a minute and wait for me there. I shan't be long.'

So out I went out into the street again (quite thankfully too, I must admit) and pretended to look at some leather jackets. I was immediately surrounded by all these guys trying to sell me their gear. I'm no use at this haggling game or getting rid of them politely, but tried to maintain a dignified silence.

Then I heard a shriek. It was his nibs hot-footing it out of the shop and puffing a bit though he hadn't far to go.

'What? What's happened?' I took hold of him. He was shaking.

'Quick,' he said. 'Let's get going.'

He took my arm and pulled me down the hill. We wasn't being stared at in a friendly way by the natives.

'Back to the hotel then?' I asked.

'No,' he said. 'Down to the port. I told you we were going to the port, didn't I?'

'What was all that about?' I asked.

'Oh nothing. He was trying to rip me off.'

'D'you know him then?'

'No. of course not. How could I?'

'Well, you seemed to recognise the shop, didn't ya? You went straight in, didn't ya?'

'Made a mistake,' he said all lofty, like, and said no more.

So off we trot down the hill like a couple of prats. He holding me arm and I, the big guy, protecting him from God knows what. We get to the port and turn right along the seafront. It got a bit quieter like, and he slowed down a little, but kept looking over his shoulder.

'Who's chasing you?' I asked.

'No one,' he snapped. 'Why should anyone chase me?'

'Then why are you behaving suspicious like?' I went on.

'Let's just enjoy the view,' he muttered.

Not much of a view in my opinion. There was the sea of course, and the railway line, and the road with cars screaming past. But apart from that it was peaceful enough, I suppose. The Rif Hotel hove into view.

'Churchill stayed there,' he said. I wasn't really interested. Before my time, like. I think he wanted to tell some story about the good old days, but I wasn't in the mood. Suddenly he crossed the road, saying 'Let's have a swim.'

He was certainly unpredictable, that's for sure.

'Haven't brought me things,' I said.

'What things?'

'Me swimming trunks and that.'

'Never mind,' he said, and walked over the railway line onto the beach. There was a line of beach bars – or bathing establishments, as me mum used to call them. Them places with places to change, a loo if you're lucky, and soft drinks and sandwiches. Some of them looked quite posh though. We was walking along the sand, when he stopped at this place called Ali's Bar. Probably the worst of the lot. The hut had only just got a roof, and there was a nasty pong of old toilets with no flushing facilities.

'I'll ask in here,' he said, and went inside. I followed him in dutiful like, and once again was told to wait outside. The sun was beating down on my head, and I wished I'd brought a straw hat or something. I like the sun, but this was something else. I was beginning to get uncomfortable, being hot and that. There was nowhere in the shade unless I sat in one of the deckchairs under the straw umbrellas, but you'd have to pay for them and I didn't know if we was stopping or not. There was an awful lot of sand with the sea miles away – at least one hundred yards. So I wandered about, but not going too far from where his nibs was.

Time went on. I began to get worried. At the risk of getting a bollocking from his nibs, I decided to poke my nose inside the hut and check he was all right.

He wasn't there. Where the hell had he gone to? There was this kid sitting outside the door smoking a fag. Couldn't have been more than twelve, neither. What 's the world coming to, I wonder?

'You speak English?' I addressed him politely.

The kid considered this for a while, and then hawked up a load of phlegm like me Dad used to. 'Course,' he said.

'Have you seen my friend?' I asked.

'Who, mister?'

'The old bloke. He came with me.'

The kid eyed me and smoked on. 'No,' he said finally.

'You was here when we came,' I insisted.

'No,'

Things was getting serious. Here I was on a ruddy beach miles from home, not speaking the lingo, and I'd lost my lord and master at the first go. Things were not good. I gave the kid what I hoped was a dirty look, and walked into the hut.

'No, mister.' The boy suddenly came to life.' No go in there.'

'I'm in,' I said. ' Whad'ya gonna do about it?'

He ran in after me. It was dark inside, but when my eyes got used to it, I saw the place was bigger than I first thought.

'Where is he?' I looked and felt quite tough at that moment. Perhaps because I was scared.

The kid considered this for a minute, smoked his last and threw the butt out of the door. 'Gone to hotel,' he said.

'What hotel?'

'Rif. You know?'

'The Rif Hotel?' What the hell was he doing going to the hotel, and how did he get there? 'Don't be daft,' I said to the kid. He didn't get the drift.

'Why did he go?'

The boy shrugged.

'Who with?'

'Boss man,' the boy said. and pointed to a large poster advertising lemonade in Arabic. I looked at the poster, then realised it was nailed to a door at the back.

'Here?' I pointed. The kid nodded, filched another packet of smokes from under the bar, and went out into the sun.

The door opened easily, and I found myself facing the railway again, and right across the street was The Rif Hotel. Jesus, I said to myself, this job is not for me. When I see his nibs again, I'm going to resign. I took my life into my hands and crossed the railway and the road without causing too much disturbance, although one or two car horns was kicking up a fuss for some reason or other.

I went into the Rif.

Quite impressive it was too inside. All Moorish design and that. Marble halls and dark. Not as nice as our hotel, I thought, but good just the same. At least it was cool, with the marble floors and air-conditioning and that. There was no sign of them in the hall. That would've been too easy, I suppose. I looked around, but everything was quiet. A few people lounging about smoking and drinking, but no sign of our Dickie. I found the swimming pool at the back. It was small surrounded by high walls, which made me hot and claustrophobic. But the tourists lying about was all comfy and content.

No sign of him though.

I went back into the hall not knowing what to do. I was feeling guilty too. He had taken me on to protect him, and I hadn't done much so far. I supposed I thought he was joking and that, and that there wouldn't be anything for me to do. I'm real stupid sometimes. I lit a fag and thought for a bit. Some kind of effort was required.

Then I had one of me brilliant ideas. I wandered over casual like to reception, where a snotty-nosed individual was fiddling with some papers.

'Good morning,' I said in my best accent. Think of Dickie.

The guy looked up. 'Yes? Sir?' he added reluctantly.

'I wonder if you could help me,' I went on smoothly. 'Have you seen a tall, rather plump gentlemen come in here a few minutes ago?'

The man sighed. 'We have a lot of guests, sir. I can't remember - '

'Oh but you would if you saw this gentleman,' I pressed on. 'Very distinguished looking, English, with white hair, in his seventies. He came in with a man from the beach bar opposite. Name of Ali, I think.'

The man had put down his papers, and was staring at me. 'And who might you be, sir?'

I swallowed hard. 'I'm his son. I seem to have lost him for the moment.'

The man's face changed. 'Oh,' he said. 'His son? Well, sir, they've gone upstairs to meet someone.'

Time to push my luck. 'I know that, my good man.' I'd heard that in an old film and thought it was impressive. 'Please tell me the room number.'

The guy looked uncertain. 'I'll just ring through,' he said.

'Don't bother, my good man,' I continued grandly. 'The room number, if you please.'

I was beginning to enjoy speaking this way, although it was tiring and a bit of a strain.

The guy looked at me uncertain, and opened his mouth to say something. I looked at him in my most aristocratic fashion. All those old films on telly was coming in useful.

'223,' he said finally.

'Second floor, I presume?' I finished, but didn't wait for an answer. I went as fast as dignity would allow to the lift, which luckily was open, and whizzed up to the second floor. Room 223 stared me in the face. I listened for a moment and heard loud noises of shouting and that. His nibs was in trouble. I banged hard on the door.

The noises stopped, and I banged again. The door opened a crack, and a nasty looking individual with a big moustache eyed me suspiciously. 'Yes?' he said. His nibs came into view. He was white and frightened, and clutching a large holdall.

'Help,' he cried.

I played my trump card again. 'Hello Dad,' I said, and pushed my way through into the room.

His nibs gulped, but didn't speak. 'You his son?' The moustache looked at me.

'Course I am,' I said. 'Come on, Dad. Time you had your nap.'

A wan smile would best describe the face as he moved to leave the room. The moustache took his arm. 'A minute,' he spat out nastily.

'Dad' got back on his dignity: 'I paid you your price, so now we're leaving,' he said. His sweaty hand grasped my arm.

'I don't think so,' threatened the moustache.

It was at that moment I felt enough was enough. Ali was emerging from the bathroom and taking up position with the moustache.

'Go on, Dad,' I said and pushed him out of the room. I turned and faced the two men. 'What's your problem?' I spat.

'Your father owes money.'

'I don't think so. You heard him. He paid you what you asked.'

'Price gone up.'

'Since when?'

'Since now.' Moustache was getting nasty. He shoved me against the wall. 'You pay price.'

That did it. 'Piss off,' I said, forgetting my aristocratic manners, and shoved him back. I was now facing the door and could see our Dickie looking anxiously at me from the corridor. 'Get the lift, Dad,' I shouted, and he scuttled away. The two men were looking very nasty indeed, and were coming straight at me. I launched a straight one at the moustache's face, and heard something crack. A quick karate kick in the balls settled Ali for a while. Another punch on the stomach to finish off the moustache, and I was out of there. Slamming the door shut, I raced to the lift where Dickie was keeping the lift door open. Thank God it whizzed down to the lobby quick as you like, and we was walking dignified like out into the sunshine.

A taxi was coming and I stepped into the road to make sure he'd stop. I bundled Dickie in, and we was off in time to see the receptionist come out and wave his arms. But we were away.

Back at the El Minzah, I helped him out and up to his room. He was panting still, and very pale. I plonked him down on the bed, and sat opposite him.

'Right, Dickie me lad, start talking. What the hell are you up to?'

CHAPTER THREE

Maggie

Still no word from Steve. It's been two days now, and he promised to phone as soon as he could. I know I shouldn't be worrying: he's a big boy and all that, but I'm not even sure where he's gone. He just said Morocco and Tangier, but he didn't know the name of the hotel or anything. I've been looking out of the window and thinking of him in the sunshine. Here, it's raining as usual. Sometimes I don't know why I left Edinburgh; the weather down here isn't much better. And that's really the reason I left: to get away from that terrible north wind that blows round the Waverley Steps.

No, that wasn't the reason. It was Ian, the bastard. He was a bastard literally, but I meant how he treated me. My sister Janet came round to see me earlier tonight, and it brought it all back. What I'd been through with Ian.

Janet and I come from Edinburgh. She's a couple of years older than me, but we don't look much alike, except for the red hair. She married five years ago and came south here to Ashford. After Ian and I separated, she suggested I come here and make a fresh start. She and Andy, her husband, have been brilliant. When I lost my baby and broke up from Ian, they put me up in their flat till I got myself sorted. Janet's a nurse at the William

Harvey hospital here in Ashford, where her thick Scottish accent amuses and infuriates the patients and staff. Janet is a strong, but pessimistic character; who always sees the worst of everything. Her Andy had gone out with his mates, so she came round with a bottle ready for a chat. She thinks Steve's up to no good, and I must say I have to agree with her. I don't want to, but I do.

'You don't know where he's gone for sure, why he's gone, or who this old man is. I've never heard of anything so weird,' she summed up while pouring the bottle of red.

'He's a kind of minder' I replied weakly.

'Steve cannae mind himsel', let alone a stranger. He thinks of himsel' all the time. You ken that fine.' She swigged the wine down, and I followed suit. She went on in like vein for quite a time and I was getting pretty tearful.

'What are ye going to do about it?' Janet demanded.

I broke down at that, and Janet was immediately contrite. 'I'm sorry hen.' She gave me a hug. 'I didnae mean - '

'Yes you did,' I sniffed, tearfully. 'But you're right. When he comes back - '

'If he comes back,' Janet had to interject.

'When he comes back,' I went on firmly, 'I'll have it out with him. Either he's gotta be completely honest with me, or we go our separate ways.'

Having said that and thought of the dramatic consequences, I began to blubber like a baby. Janet's strong arms took me to her bosom. She's a pessimist all right, but her heart's in the right place. She's always stood by me and looked after me, just like an elder sister should. Sometimes I think I lean on her too much.

She patted my back like she was burping a baby. 'You just stop your greetin' hen. If you won't tell him, just hand him over to me. I'll sort him for you.'

'Thanks, Janet, but I can manage,' I sobbed. 'I'll give him what for all right.'

At this point the phone rang. It was Steve.

STEVE

'How dare you call me Dickie,' Richard Grayson said with an attempt at dignity.

'Come off it,' I grinned. 'You can't get on your high horse now. What are you up to?'

'Not up to anything.'

'So that nasty scene in the hotel was just a bit of fun, I suppose.'

'A misunderstanding, that's all.'

I lit a cigarette, which annoyed him, but he hadn't the strength to say anything. 'Look, Dickie old mate,' I said, 'you took me on as your minder or whatever. You never said nothing about why or what. If you want me to continue with this, you've gotta let me in on it. Whatever it is.'

He sighed. 'Later,' he said. 'I'm very tired. I'll tell you later.'

'Not good enough, mate. Tell me now.'

He sighed again, and shook his head. 'Mr Jackman - ' he began.

'Steve,' I put in.

'Stephen - '

'Steve,' I repeated.

His face softened, and he smiled at me all relaxed. Amazing the difference in the old geezer when he smiles. He looks quite human and almost loveable.

'Go on,' I prompted.

'Well - Steve - it's nothing really. Nothing that need concern you greatly. I'm just buying a bit of dark Moroccan cannabis, that's all.'

'I thought so. You old slyboots you. I thought it was something like that. So, you're a drug runner, are you?.'

'I'm nothing of the sort,' he said indignantly. 'I don't touch drugs.'

'What's pot then?'

'Therapeutic,' he answered loftily. 'All I'm doing is buying a couple of packets, then we take them to Gibraltar and sell it.'

'We?'

'Me then. You're not involved.'

'I see. So that's what you want me for. To get you out of messes like what you was into today.'

'Not at all,' he said. 'That was an accident.'

'So what do you want me for?'

'This morning was an accident,' he went on oblivious. 'We had agreed a price, but when we got upstairs they decided to up the ante.'

'Up the ante? You've done this before, haven't you?'

'This is a minor sale. Nothing big. We'll take it to Gib tomorrow.'

'You're taking a lot for granted, ain't you? What makes you think I approve of these criminal activities?'

He smiled again. 'Steve – dear boy – don't play the innocent with me. And don't tell me you've never partaken of the weed.'

I must admit I'm partial to a bit of blow now and then. Can't understand the fuss they make about it. Better than lager any day. 'I suppose,' I looked stern, 'that's why you picked me. You was exploiting my weaknesses. I should never have said I'd been in trouble with the police – even though it was nothing really.'

He laughed. 'I love it when you come over all moral,' he said.

I didn't know what he meant really. 'And' I said, 'what was all that rumpus in the shop on the way down to the port?'

'Oh that?' Dickie laughed. 'Usually the cannabis has either been left in the shop or on the beach at Ali's. Only now the gang has split up, and the shop people run their own show. And I was unaware of this.'

'So why were you frightened?'

'I wasn't frightened.' He was on his high horse again. 'They just knew I'd have a lot of cash on me, so they made a move to get it. That's when I shouted for you.'

I couldn't help smiling: his attempt at smuggling looked a bit cack-handed to me. Then I stopped smiling when I realised I was now part of it.

'Anyway,' our Dickie was looking perky again, 'you were a great help. In fact, I thought you were rather magnificent.'

Put like that, I could hardly carry on looking stuffy, could I?

'Come on,' he got to his feet. 'Let's go downstairs and have a slap-up lunch, with a nice bottle of champers. You can tell me about your heroic intervention, and how you found me.' He looked at me almost with affection. 'You really did come to my rescue, Steve. And I thank you for that, very much indeed.'

We went downstairs like we was two old buddies. The afternoon passed me by in a haze of heat and champers.

MAGGIE

It's getting worse. He rang up all right, but sounded halfcut. I got some jumbled story about a day by the sea, that it was hot and they'd had a big lunch. Janet was still with me, and kept mouthing questions for me to ask, but I couldn't understand him at all. Said he was off to Gibraltar the next morning – sounded quite the experienced traveller.

'What'ya going to Gibraltar for?'

Silly question really, and I got a silly answer.

'Tourism, of course,' he replied. 'Everybody does a day trip to Gib.'

Gib? You'd think he'd been there for years.

'When are you coming home?' I asked. I must have sounded a bit plaintive, ''Cos he sighed heavily and said he didn't know, as if he were talking to a child.

'Must go now,' he said. 'It costs the earth to phone. Ring you soon.'

'That means you're away for a while then?'

'Don't know. Honest. Speak to you soon.' And with that he hung up.

Janet had a wee belch. 'Doesnae sound good to me,' she said.

I didn't want to agree with her; I wanted to say everything was fine and hunky-dory, but I couldn't. So I said nothing.

'Thought you were going to give him what for,' she went on.

'I will. When he gets back. It's useless having a row on the phone.'

'And when will that be, may I ask?'

'Soon, I expect. It's just a short trip. They're going to Gibraltar tomorrow.'

'Gibraltar, is it? Living the life of Reilly, is he? What else did he say?'

'Not much. I think he'd been drinking.'

'Right,' said Janet. 'That settles it. I'm away for another bottle. He's not the only one who can enjoy himsel'. Come on hen, we're away to get a drink in.'

I didn't really feel like it. Janet saw my face and softened a bit.

'Come on, Maggie,' she said. 'Remember when Ian used to have his benders and leave you at home all night? You're not going to let this happen again, are you?'

'Steve's no' like Ian,' I had to defend him. 'Steve's away on holiday, that's all. There's no comparison.'

'There is from where I'm sitting. But please yoursel'. Are you coming oot for a bevvy or no?'

Might as well, I thought. I must say there's nothing worse than hearing your partner's having a good time, while you're moping at home miserable as sin. So I nodded, and got my coat. It was raining as usual, just to add to things.

STEVE

So we're on this kind of ferryboat to Gibraltar. It's a very hot day, and his nibs is sweating like a pig, whether from the heat or fear I don't know. He's got his grass stashed away in his holdall, and I'm scared stiff. When he said he'd got a couple of packets, I thought he meant like what you buy in the street. It turns out they're two bags the size of Tesco's potato sacks.

I've never been into smuggling before, but I must say it gives you a bit of a buzz. The trip took longer than I thought, and by the time we were close to the Rock, my stomach was playing me up. Dunno if it was last night's food or what, but foreign fish is not for me. Anyway, I'd gone to the bog twice, and believe you me, bog is the right name for it. The boat was packed with tourists and locals and Moroccans going about their business, though I can't think what that could be.

As I came out of the loo for the third time, Dickie was looking for me anxiously. 'What have you been up to for goodness sake?' He was nervy and cross. 'I've been looking for you everywhere.'

I told him.

'Oh, well,' he said. 'You'd better get accustomed to food apart from your usual fish and chips.'

'It was the fish, and it wasn't cod neither.'

The boat docked, and we joined the queue of people lining up to get off. Disembark, as Dickie was to correct me. He was getting good at that. Whatever I said, he'd correct me, as if it wasn't my language as well.

'Him and his bloody grammar and all,' I muttered rebelliously as we approached the Customs Hall.

Suddenly his nibs saw one of the Customs Officers and panicked. 'Oh God,' he whispered, 'I know this one. He searched me the last time. I don't know why he's so suspicious of me. I look completely innocent.'

The last time? How many times had he done this? There wasn't no time to ask him, as we was approaching far too fast for my liking. He thinks he looks innocent – anyone more bizarre than my Dickie would be hard to beat. He was wearing an old-fashioned cotton suit that was all creased in the heat; a silk tie half way round his neck, and a Panama hat. He looked straight out of Casablanca. The film I mean, not the place.

The Customs Officer registered Dickie's approach while checking some Moroccans in front. For all I know they was smuggling in kilos of heroin. Dickie dropped his holdall. 'Pick it up, there's a good lad,' he said, and sailed past the Moroccans and into Customs.

He was stopped, of course, and searched, but half-heartedly I thought. There weren't many places he could be carrying anything in that thin suit. 'Back again are we sir?' I heard the Customs man say to Dickie.

'Sentimental journey,' our Dickie replied. ' I was stationed here during the war, you know.'

'Really?' said the man. 'My father was here too. Wright, his name was. Private Grenville Wright.'

'Really?' Dickie's voice faded away. 'I don't think -'

Meanwhile I was strolling through with the holdall, which weighed a ton. I couldn't believe I was doing this. I was actually running drugs, and I hadn't even been asked. He was in for it and no mistake. I walked on ahead for a bit then sat down at a bar on the quayside, beside some posh looking yachts. He puffed up to me.

'Well done, Steve,' he said. 'You did well.'

'Are you kidding?' I said. 'We never agreed this. We never said I was to be involved. You promised -'

'Well done all the same,' he said, nervously looking about him. 'We'll discuss this later. Meanwhile I still have some business to do. '

With that some geezer in a blazer and yachting cap surfaced on this big yacht by the bar, and waved to Dickie.

'How clever of you to know where to stop,' said his nibs and scrambled on board. 'Wait here for me,' he mouthed and disappeared below.

My heart was still pounding at things that was happening all too fast. I don't think I can do this. I don't think I'm suited. He never told me nothing about smuggling and getting involved. I lit another cigarette, and swigged down the beer. It made me feel worse. Why had I ordered beer? And me with the runs. I've got to get out of this. When he comes back, we'll have to have a talk.

About twenty minutes went by, and I was thinking this was going to be a repeat of the Rif Hotel business, when up his head popped, all smiles. 'Come on in, Steve,' he waved. 'It's cooler down below.'

I got up to go, then realised I'd got no money on me. Only Moroccan Dinars. I explained this to the barman, who spoke English (at least we was in a civilised country), and said I'd pay when I got back from the yacht. I was a bit surprised he didn't raise no objections like, but he smiled and said OK.

I climbed on board the yacht, thinking that at least there'd be a loo on board, and hoped that nothing else nasty was going to happen.

RICHARD

I must say I've changed my mind about young Steve. He may be brash and loud, but his heart's in the right place. He certainly came up trumps at the Rif: I didn't let him know how scared I was. And he's not so stupid as I thought. Fancy thinking up that story about my being his father. The funny thing is that he has a look of me when I was his age. I was never the butch macho type that he makes out to be – there weren't any tattoos or earrings in my day, but he has the same smile I like to think I had at his age. And I remember how I could use that to devastating advantage. I have the feeling he does the same thing. He pretended to be angry when I made him carry the holdall into Gib, but I could see that underneath he was really enjoying it.

When I got to Eric's yacht, the Annabella II, I was feeling hot and nervous: not at my best. One is always at one's worst when one wants to make a good impression. He greeted me civilly enough, and poured me a welcome glass of ice-cold champers. My mind went back to that film – *Ice Cold In Alex* – when during the desert war in Egypt all they could think of was reaching civilisation, i.e. Alexandria, and having an ice-cold beer. My thoughts wandered to my time in the war with Eric, and that bloody sun, that blistering heat, and the fear.

'You all right, old man?' Eric's voice brought me back.

'Yes, fine,' I replied untruthfully. I was really suffering from the heat. I should be used to it too after enduring it all through the war.

'Did you get it?' Eric's voice broke into my thoughts again.

'Yes, of course.' I showed him the stuff, which he sniffed like a police dog. He went to a desk drawer in the saloon and brought back a wad of notes.

'Better count it,' he said with a smile.

'After all these years? Don't be silly.' I stuffed the notes into my pocket and rose to go.

'Who's your friend?' he asked.

'What friend?' I said stupidly.

'Your young man waiting for you outside.'

'Oh, 'I said,' just a casual acquaintance.'

'I don't think so,' he laughed. 'I was watching you two working your way through Customs. He seemed to be doing the dirty work. Not you.'

'Oh well,' I said lamely.

'Bring him aboard. I'd like to meet him.'

I didn't want him getting his hands on my Steve. 'That's not necessary. We have to go now. We're going on a coach trip round the Rock.'

'Bollocks,' Eric said. 'You've seen enough of the Rock to last you a lifetime. That's the last thing you'd want to do. Bring him aboard. I've got an idea. Perhaps we can work together.'

'You and Steve? Not if I've got anything to do with it.'

'Don't get so jealous, Richard old man,' he said smoothly. 'I wouldn't dream of stealing your – Steve, is it? – from you. But I have got an idea. At least let me meet him. If nothing else we can have a drink before you go.'

I didn't want to offend him. He was my oldest friend after all. 'All right then,' I said unwillingly. 'I'll call him in.'

The heat was stifling as I went on deck. I saw Steve sitting there at the bar. He looked vulnerable somehow. I felt quite protective of him, although he was the one who was supposed to be protecting me.

He caught me looking at him, and I called to him to come aboard.

STEVE

I was feeling really bad by now, my stomach don't go with foreign food and that. Anyway, down we go into the saloon or whatever you call it. It wasn't half posh neither. All mahogany and brass handles. Just like you see in them Bond films. And air-conditioned too, thank God. There's this guy standing by the bar, giving me the once-over. Another poofter I reckon, one of Dickie's cronies. He's all suntan, and gold watch and white teeth, and not a day below seventy, I'll be bound.

Out comes the brown hand with a gold ring and liver stains to shake me hand – quite firmly too, I was surprised to notice. 'So you're Steve,' he says, the white teeth in evidence.

'That's me,' I said, stomach lurching. 'Can I use your toilet please?'

Dickie frowned at me, as if I'd let him down or something. I grinned back and tried to make me usual dignified exit. When I got back, they was sitting side by side hatching some plot I was sure. Dickie got up when he saw me. 'Steve,' he said, 'I'd like you to meet my old friend, Sir Eric Davies.'

Oh, I'm with the nobs all right.

'Please to meet ya, I'm sure.' I couldn't understand why they both smiled at that. 'What will you have to drink, Steve?' said our Eric.

'Nothing thanks,' I was feeling real miserable. 'I've got the trots, and don't feel well at all.'

'Oh dear,' he said. 'I've got just the thing for you.' And disappeared into what looked like a kind of kitchen. Back he came with a glass of orange juice and an evil looking pill. 'Here, take this.' He handed me the pill and glass. 'That'll buck you up in no time.'

I looked at Dickie for a bit of comfort. Tell the truth, my mind was on the white slave traffic. I was trying to remember if it applied to good-looking blokes like yours truly.

'I don't like orange juice,' I said.

'Best thing for you, my boy. You need the vitamins.'

I was in no state to argue; anything was better than the trots. I took the pill and swallowed it down in one.

'Sit down, old boy,' this guy waved me to a sofa thing. 'You'll be right as rain in two ticks.'

I sat down suspicious like, and wondered if I'd ever get back to England and home.

RICHARD

Steve didn't look well at all. He came aboard the yacht looking half dead, and disappeared into the loo for hours. I did so want him to make a good impression, and Eric was being exceptionally kind. He gave Steve some sort of pill for his diarrhoea, which silenced him even more. He sank into the sofa and refused to say a word. Eric kept looking at him, not knowing whether to include him in the conversation. Eventually he gave up, and addressed himself solely to me. I've known Eric all my life. We were, in fact, at school together, and then the war – I was a subaltern, and he was a captain. Always ahead of me was Eric.

We sat out most of the war together in Gibraltar, except for the last bit in the desert. People at home thought we had a cushy posting, but it was far from that. It was boring and claustrophobic, cooped up on the Rock for four years with no leave. Most of the work consisted of endless tunnelling of the Rock, the rubble from which was used to build and then extend the airstrip. All this was done under the far from benevolent eye of the Governor, Lord Gort, who had bright ideas like ordering the men to whitewash the coal heap so that the royal eyes of the visiting Duke of Gloucester wouldn't be offended by nasty black stuff. I remember an English newspaper printed a photo of us sunning ourselves on the beach at Catalan Bay, as if we were on permanent holiday. That nearly caused a riot when it reached us. Imagine all those men virtually imprisoned and hardly a woman in sight, except for a few Wrens and nurses, who were kept segregated in the 'Wrenery'. All right for me – I had a relatively good time, though one had to be careful. Straights could turn nasty with post-coital guilt. But I must say that applied more to visiting sailors and the like: there was an extraordinary camaraderie amongst the men all through that dismal time. True affection and love was frequent between the most macho of men, although they would have been appalled to have their feelings classified as such. But their gentler side would surface often. And things did improve when General Mason-MacFarlane replaced Gort.

Eric, like most of the men, suffered a lot. He was a ladies man if ever there was one. In those days he was strikingly handsome, and I had quite a crush on him. He never knew, of course – his mind was always on the ladies. I just used to gaze on that blond sunburned face, and worship silently. He was a good friend though, and we spent a lot of time together. He always managed to get himself invited to Government House or the Rock Hotel when something interesting was going on. I never did. It was he who got to dance with Vivien Leigh, although he did manage to introduce me to Noel Coward once.

After the war we lost track of each other. I had met my dear Philip by then, and my whole life revolved round him. It wasn't until the early seventies that Eric and I bumped into each other in Capri. I was with my friends, and he with his. He still had the old Annabella even then (he was to sell it soon after, and buy the yacht he has now – the Annabella II, which was a smaller version, but still impressive enough). It was anchored off the Marina Piccola near the Christina and the Revlon. The Annabella was not in the same class as those two yachts, but it was still grand enough for people to ask whose it was. We had dinner together one night – hardly a quiet affair. There were about twenty others present, but afterwards, we went for a stroll along the Via Tragara away from the crowds, and caught up with each other's history since the war.

I knew he had married, and married megabucks as they say. The papers had been disapproving: it wasn't cricket to marry a rich American heiress, even though Eric had done quite well for himself in the Stock Market. There was even more disapprobation when his wife - Claudia - died suddenly of a fever. The tabloids were particularly sniffy, I remember, probably because they disapproved of anyone inheriting millions. In fact the reverse was true - he hardly got a penny. There was something about Claudia's money being in trust for their only daughter, so that he got the yacht, and the house in London, but no hard cash. Anyway, one could hardly lose sleep over his financial difficulties, when one's own were in a much more parlous state.

We were smoking a cigarette and looking at the Faraglioni in the moonlight when he told me what he was up to. I was shocked at first, as one is, but soon changed my tune. Contraband, of course. It was easy in the early seventies: there were no Customs patrols of any significance in the Neapolitan area (the Camorra took care of that), so he was indulging in a little light smuggling to top up his income. He had begun with cigarettes and liquor, but got entangled with the Camorra, who intended to keep the monopoly on that to themselves. The Mafiosi of Naples were not a friendly bunch, and had just warned him off their patch in a most unsavoury, but convincing, manner.

He told me that he was going to make Gibraltar his base, and there take stock of the marijuana trade, and would I like to help? Smuggling cannabis out of Morocco usually went from Ceuta across the Strait to Algeciras. But he had thought up a way into Spain from Tangier via Gib. My finances were in no great shape at that time: I had been an MP for several years, and a very good one at that, when suddenly the bottom had fallen out of my world. I was accused of taking money in return for favours. Quite untrue, of course. That was in 1963, when the Government was beset by sex scandals and the Profumo case. My affair with Philip, the love of my life, had been rumbled, and they didn't want any other skeletons in the cupboard. So I resigned, and was making do with one or two minor directorships, which were hardly sufficient to keep me off the streets, as my mother used to say. I particularly enjoyed travelling, first class at that, and that required more money then I was making.

Years ago I had met an old American who came to Capri every year for three months, staying at one of the best hotels. He had retired long since, and I wondered how he could afford it. One night after a particularly alcoholic evening, he told me his secret. Although he had been in the rag trade, he loved art, and had acquired a knowledge of painting through the years. On his way home from Capri, he would go to Paris, buy a couple of canvases, take them back to the States rolled up at the bottom of a suitcase, and sell them for nearly twice what he had paid. This fired me with a similar idea. I had always loved gems and fine craftsmanship, so I taught myself the rudiments. I had several acquaintances in antiques and jewellery, who filled in the gaps, and gave me valuable advice. Thus I went all over, buying a gem here, a piece of jade there, and bringing them back to the UK to sell. I soon found out that Customs could cut your profits seriously, so I began to 'forget' I had something to declare, and just walked through the Green with the stuff in my pocket. I had various ploys to beat them (all of which the Customs consider elementary these days) – my favourite being to put diamonds in my duty-free vodka, and other small stones enveloped in a wad of sterling currency. Although I had a healthy respect for the Customs men and their work, at bottom I disapproved of it, holding the view that what I bought abroad was paid for with my money that had already been subjected to income tax. So I began my life of light-hearted smuggling. Eric's suggestion of working in Morocco therefore appealed to me, as long as I didn't have to do it too often.

So I accepted his offer. That was the beginning of a long partnership – well, not really a partnership, as Eric was always the boss, and I was just a tiny piece of his mosaic. At the beginning, he used me and other contacts to smuggle in his cannabis. Different techniques were used – never the same way twice. Sometimes I went in by ferry and sometimes by plane; sometimes with a partner as stooge to create a diversion, and sometimes alone. But then it grew into a big hard drug operation, which I preferred not to know about, and he became a powerful drug baron. I really wasn't into that kind of thing, and had become less and less involved as it became more and more dangerous. Still, he was good to work for. Controls at Tangier and Gib were quite lax in those days, and easy to circumvent once one had learnt a few tricks. Looking back, I realise I must have been extremely lucky, but I suppose smugglers never imagine they will be caught. Now things were different: controls were strict, and my face had become too well known for this caper. This was going to be my last time, and I decided to do it solo by ferry. But as we neared the Customs, I began to think of all the narrow escapes I'd had and I panicked at the last moment, and shifted all responsibility onto Steve. Never again. It was a reprehensible and cowardly act, and I was thoroughly ashamed of myself.

Eric still enjoyed the danger, however, in spite of, or perhaps because of his tragedies: his beloved daughter had married some man in the City. Everything was going well for them, when she died giving birth to Yolanda, his granddaughter, who in turn inherited all of Claudia's wealth. The money was put in trust, and Eric was in charge of her upbringing and education. When she grew up, she married when she was 19 and divorced two years later. She remarried last year, and was now on her second divorce. He was reporting on her latest exploits when Steve suddenly jerked himself to his feet, looking like his old self.

He gave us one of his grins. 'Hi there,' he said. 'What's up?'

STEVE

They looked so posh and upper class, but I'm as good as them..Only I don't feel that when I'm with them. I get this inferior feeling and I don't like it. They're a right pair of villains, muttering away to each other. I could see the Eric guy tying up what Dickie had brought over together with a smaller packet – I didn't like to think what was inside that. He was making it into a neat parcel, covered in waterproof material, and tied with cord. Why waterproof I didn't know or care much; I just wanted out of there. When they saw I was awake and meself again, Eric put the parcel out of sight, and Dickie clucked at me like an old hen.

'Well, Steve, feeling better?' Dickie cried.

Physically, I certainly was. God knows what that guy had given me, but I felt a new man, until I realized something odd was happening: we was moving. The bloody boat was on the move.

'Oh my God, what's happening?' I rushed to a sort of porthole.

'Now then, Steve, calm down.' Dickie took my arm and pulled me back. 'We're only going for a little jaunt round the Rock.'

'What for?' I cried. I was sure I was being abducted. Africa was just across the road, so to speak.

'We're only going for a quick swim.' The Eric guy was being smooth.

'I don't want a swim. I want to go home.' I felt a right Charlie, talking like a child, but I was scared shitless.

Dickie managed to calm me down. He was actually very sympathetic, as if he understood how panicky I was. He smiled his paternal smile, and said: 'Don't worry Steve, my boy, I'll look after you.'

I almost believed him.

'Come and sit down,' said the Eric guy, and took me by the arm. I didn't like that much, but on the other hand, I could hardly shove him off now, could I? 'Fancy some champagne?' He was pouring the stuff out like there was no tomorrow.

I was sick of champagne, sick of drink altogether. I had a strong urge for hot milk and bed. Must be getting old. But I refused politely, and watched them slurp the stuff down like they was celebrating or something.

Dickie suggested we go on deck and get some fresh air. It was a good idea, actually. The boat was going at a fair lick creating a welcome breeze. The Rock did look impressive as we swept round it. I could see Spain in the distance. 'Is that where we're going?' I pointed to a sandy beach with a hotel in the shade of the Rock, and lots of people swimming and that.

'A bit further I think. That's Catalan Bay,' Dickie added helpfully.

'That's where I used to swim during the war. I was stationed here, you know.'

'Cushy job you had then, didn't you? ' I said. He looked quite hurt at that. I suppose the war was pretty bad wherever you was. 'Was he with you then?' I nodded toward Eric, who was conferring with one of the crew.

'Yes, we were together most of the time.' His eyes took on a misty look. Funny old geezer he is, and all.

The boat was swinging away from the Rock, and the funny feeling came back to my stomach. 'Now what?' I cried in a panic.

'It's all right, Steve,' soothed Dickie. 'Eric's decided to show you a bit of the coastline of Spain. It's very pretty along here. You'll like it, I'm sure.'

I wasn't sure at all. I was being kidnapped, yet in a civilised way. I didn't know what I could do about it neither. We was belting along that coast, obviously going somewhere definite. This was no joyride I could tell.

It was quite a while later when I felt the boat losing speed and I could see we was approaching a small town with a marina or harbour. Quite nice it was too. I was longing to stretch me legs on dry land.

'This is Puerto Banus,' Eric came up to us. 'We'll anchor here for a while so that you can have a swim.'

'But I don't want -'

He was away back to the crew, giving orders and that. I looked at Dickie. 'Don't worry, Steve,' he said. 'Just enjoy yourself. Let's have a swim.'

The water was deep and blue and very cool looking. Swimming trunks appeared from nowhere, and we went below to change, though why we did that I don't know. There was only men on board.

Anyway, Dickie and I clambered down the steps that had been lowered and I dived in while Dickie splashed about after me. Looking back, that must have been one of the best swims I ever had. I'd never swum in deep water before: it was so cool and clean and blue and that. It made you feel real good. I did my duty with Dickie and saw that he didn't drown or nothing. Actually, he was quite a good swimmer considering his age – very elegant crawl and that. He soon got our of breath though, and clambered back on board. I watched him disappear to the other side of the boat. I felt great – sort of weightless like, and when I dived under the surface into that deep blue, it was kind of spiritual.

Several motor boats were zooming about near us: obviously the locals and tourists had come up to have a look. Then I noticed a police boat speeding our way, and I didn't like the look of that. Police to me means trouble. I was several yards in front of the bows and swimming round to the seaward side of the yacht, when I saw Eric talking to a guy standing up in a dinghy. Another guy was stowing away what must be the stuff that Dickie – or rather I – had brought in. It was now wrapped in an innocent looking plastic bag. The bastards. So that was what it was all about.

I waved to Eric. 'Police are coming,' I shouted.

Eric looked stunned. 'Jesus,' he swore. 'What for?'

The guy in the dinghy jabbered away in Spanish and everybody started to wave and act like foreigners. 'That waterproof inside?' I pointed to the parcel.

'Yes,' Eric said.

'Right mate. Give it to me. I'm just a tourist having a swim.'

Eric looked at me amazed, and then his face lit up. Dickie was smiling behind him, nodding his approval.

They threw me the package, which was bigger than I thought. I looped the handles of the bag round my foot and tried to tread water. It was not as simple as I had imagined. I don't know, I must be crazy. When you're with thieves you act like one yourself. I swam away from the yacht looking a right pillock, pushing the bloody parcel underfoot, hoping to God it wouldn't surface.

By the time the police boat rounded the yacht and was talking to the men in the dinghy, I had managed to distance meself from the scene of the crime, and was dog-paddling about, trying to look as if I was enjoying meself. The police stayed on the yacht for a lifetime, and I was tiring rapidly. When they finally left, they made straight for me. I was shitting meself, I can tell ya. They slowed down as they neared me, and I waved at them friendly like. One of the guys waved back. 'All right señor?' he smiled.

I must have looked a real learner, flapping about the way I was. 'Yes, fine,' I replied. 'Never better.'

'You a long way out,' he said.

'I like it,' I said, trying not to look half-dead. 'Practising a new stroke for the Olympics.'

That was too much for the cop's English, but he smiled and gave me another wave, and off they went. I waited until they was nearly back on land before making me way back to the boat.

I was welcomed aboard like a hero and taken below to a hot shower and a brandy. By the time I'd got meself dry and dressed again, the boat engines were throbbing and we was on our way back.

'Well,' I began, 'of all the dirty tricks -'

'What do you mean, Steve?' We was down in the saloon again.

'You might have said -'

'You might have made a fuss,' Dickie said, slurping more champagne down his fat throat. 'As it is, you behaved like a hero. You really surpassed yourself this time, Steve, old son.'

'Nearly shit meself more like,' I muttered. He always got so friendly like at the wrong time.

'What about something to eat?' Eric asked. And I must admit I was starving. 'What would you like, Steve?'

'What have you got?'

'Whatever you like.'

Eventually I settled for real baked beans and bangers, with chips and tomatoes. Gibraltar had everything evidently. I scoffed it down and felt a lot better. 'I can't believe you did that,' I was lighting a ciggie.

'What?' asked Eric.

'That transfer at Puerto whatsit. Didn't you expect to be searched? Why didn't you have someone on watch?'

'Someone should have been on watch. They disobeyed orders. They were over on our side watching the operation. He's being disciplined,' he added grimly.

'All the same,' I said. 'You treat it too casual like.'

They looked at each other smiling. 'Not really, Steve,' said Eric. 'I have an understanding with the Police here. There shouldn't have been any trouble at all. Unfortunately, the wrong man was on duty today. My usual man was off sick. But thanks to you, we still have the stuff – I'll just have to go back tomorrow with it.'

'You mean the coppers are bent?'

They both laughed. 'Don't tell me you think all the police in Britain are squeaky clean,' chortled Dickie.

'No, of course not.' I knew this only too well. My opinion of the Bill is well known. 'Still, you never know, do you?'

'Anyway, Steve,' said Eric, 'you behaved admirably. You showed quick thinking and acted with laudable courage and competence. You knew there was more than your cannabis in that package, didn't you?'

'Guessed as much,' I growled.

'So you saved me a great deal of money and inconvenience. All of which,' he got to his feet, and went to a drawer in the desk, 'merits a just reward.' He fished out a bundle of notes. 'Please accept this with my gratitude.'

It turned out to be two hundred quid, in good old English tenners. 'Here, I can't take this,' I began, knowing bloody well I could.

'Of course, you can,' he smiled. 'Besides, I think that underneath your moral disapprobation, you really enjoyed it.'

I couldn't answer that one, neither. For it's true, I did get a bit of a kick from what I done. 'Well thanks a lot then,' I accepted graciously.

'Now then, Steve my boy,' burped Dickie. 'Sir Eric has something to ask you.'

'Oh yeh?' I didn't like the sound of that one.

Eric gave me the benefit of his choppers. 'Well, Steve,' he began. 'I have been watching you carefully...'

Oh yes?

'...and I was most impressed with how you handled things today.'

I opened my mouth to reply, but he went on: 'He also told me how you defused the potentially dangerous situation yesterday in Tangier. Things could have turned very nasty. Very nasty indeed, but for your intervention.'

'It's what I'm paid for,' I mumbled.

'You did more than in the line of duty, my boy.'

If there's one thing I hate, it's being patronised, and I could feel this coming very strongly from Eric Little by Little. Funny that, ''Cos the way Dickie talks to me is patronising all right, but somehow I know he don't mean it to be. It's just his way. Eric's got a nice line in flannel, and takes his time with it too. I was wishing he'd get to the point.

'So, my boy, I was considering taking you on full-time in our little ventures.'

'And what kind of ventures would they be now?' I asked.

'Just what you've been doing for the past few days.'

'Smuggling, you mean?'

'Yes, if you put it like that.'

'How else would you put it?' I could see Dickie frowning at me.

'I prefer contraband. It has a better ring to it.'

Why's he splitting hairs? It's against the law whatever you say, and I told him so.

'Against the law as it stands, but also very lucrative.'

'For you may be. What's in it for me?' I didn't mean to say that. I meant to refuse point-blank. I don't want no trouble with the law that's all.

Eric relaxed at that. He thought he had me hooked. 'Quite a lot, Steve, my boy. Quite a lot. I'm moving out tonight. This little caper has come to an end. There's no more future in it. Customs are getting far too nosy for my comfort...'

Pity I didn't know that before I brought his pot in.

'So I'm going to fresh fields. And I'd like you to help me.'

'How?'

'Just doing the same as now. Being a kind of courier. Only the merchandise won't be the same.'

'What merchandise?'

'Something more lucrative, Steve. More in the way of the hard stuff, as it's called.'

'You mean heroin and that?'

'Precisely, dear boy. Something more in that line.'

This was not my idea at all. Running a bit of grass was one thing, but the hard stuff was definitely out.

'No thanks,' I said. 'I want to live a little longer, thanks very much. I'm not doing nothing dangerous like that.'

'Double negative, Steve,' chipped in Dickie. 'Two negatives don't make a positive.'

'What the hell are you on about now?' I swung round at him, real mad I was.

He sighed. 'Oh, never mind.'

Eric Little by Little had had enough of me for the moment. He smiled falsely. 'Richard,' he smarmed. 'Why not take Steve on that tour of the Rock? Explain a little more clearly what I have in mind. Come back here on your way back to the ferry, and we'll have another chat. In a calmer atmosphere, I hope.'

Dickie nodded agreement, and no more was said about it till we got back to Gibraltar and docked at the marina. We said goodbye, and walked into the town.

'You certainly can have the sulks in a big way,' began Dickie, panting in the heat.

'Not sulking. Just hopping mad.'

'What about? Eric was being perfectly amiable and civil. Which is more than you were. You really must learn some manners, Steve.'

The sun was blinding hot. 'Don't you patronise me, you old bastard. I won't be patronised.'

That put a stop to any further argument till we reached the main street. It had been quite a walk, further than Dickie had realised. At least there was shade in the street, and I suddenly felt at home. There was Marks and Sparks, several English pubs and Sainsbury's and everything. We was back in civilisation.

Dickie turned into a nice looking pub. 'Let's have a drink and calm down,' he said.

We went in and ordered mineral water with ice. There was air-conditioning as well. We drank deep. He looked at me. 'Feeling better now?'

I had to grin at him. 'You've got a cheek,' I said, but friendly like.

'You're the cheeky one, my son,' he said, and looked anxious. I don't think he meant to say my son.

'Well, anyway.'

'Look, Steve, there's no point in us fighting about this, is there? If you don't want to do it, then say so. But don't take it out on me.'

He had a point there, I suppose. I nodded and finished the mineral water. 'Let's have some more,' he said, and went to the bar. When he came back, I had to have my say.

'That's all very well, and I agree with you and that,' I said, 'but you said I had to be like honest with you – so I think you should be honest with me. Fair dos and that.'

'I am being honest -'

'No, you're not. You're that cagey. I wish you wouldn't put me into things without so much as a by your leave.'

'What things?' He looked genuinely puzzled.

'You know. Passing me the grass at the last moment. Making me responsible and all. You were bang out of order there.'

'Yes. Sorry about that.' Dickie hung his head.

'Then that Eric character, putting things to me as if I was a criminal.'

'I'm sure that wasn't his intention,' Dickie began. 'It was just that he was so impressed with what you -'

'No? Well, that's how it looked to me. Anyway, I don't want no part of it, and that's flat. If I'd known that was what you wanted me for I wouldn't have come, definitely,'

Dickie looked even more amazed. 'But that's not the reason I wanted you at all,' he said. 'This is just a sideline.'

'So what did you want me for?'

'As I told you. To look after me and protect me. A job, I must say, you are fulfilling way beyond my expectations.'

'Yes, well. I still don't understand.'

'There's nothing to worry about, dear boy. If you don't want to help Sir Eric, then that's fine by me. Actually, if you must know, I've never helped with the heroin, and I don't intend to start now.'

'Really?'

'Really. And, for your information, I don't do this all that often. Maybe three or four times a year, maximum.'

'Then why egg me on like?'

'I wasn't egging you on. I just thought if you wanted to accept Eric's offer, then do so with my blessing. It was a good opportunity for you, if you wanted to go into that line of business.'

So we left it at that. We didn't do a tour of the Rock as was suggested, because it was getting late. We had to get back and catch the last ferry. Dickie decided on a taxi – he was getting real tired I could see.

'So what did you mean,' I said, on the way back to the port, 'about the double negative? What the hell's that?'

He explained. It seemed a bit pointless. 'I meant what I said, and people know what I meant, didn't they?'

'Well, yes and no, Steve. But one never stops learning, does one? You see, if you talk like that, you're putting yourself into a definite category.'

'But the way you talk puts you into a category, don't it'?

He had to smile at that. 'Look, Steve, I'm not trying to be a Professor Higgins -'

'Who?'

'The *Pygmalion story*. You know, *My Fair Lady* and all that?'

'Oh yeah. I remember the film. But she was a Cockney, and I ain't.'

He sighed. 'Never mind. It doesn't matter.'

But it did in a way. He was unsettling me somehow. I was beginning to think I didn't know nothing.

RICHARD

It's been an exhausting day. First the ferry to Gib and getting the stuff through Customs. I lost my nerve at the last moment and gave it to Steve to carry through. An unforgivable thing to do, and I repent it deeply. He feels I'm using him to do the dirty work, and I didn't mean it like that at all. I must say, though, I don't think he's as shocked as he pretends to be. Underneath that righteous facade there's a little gleam in his eye as if he secretly relishes it.

Anyway, he and Eric didn't really hit it off in spite of Steve's heroic intervention at Puerto Banus, and Steve was positively rude in the end. I managed to calm him down a bit, and we decided to go back and tell Eric we wanted no part of his plans. I paid off the taxi, and we were strolling back to the yacht when an ambulance went screaming past us, lights flashing. There was a small crowd hovering near the yacht, and I recognized one of the crew. He was a short, cheeky little Filipino, who had been with Eric for years. He was shouting hysterically and generally carrying on, as they do. I guessed who was in the ambulance and panic set in. I took hold of Steve's arm and tried to move him on.

'What's the matter with you then?' he had to ask.

'This is none of our business, Steve. Let's just get back to the ferry.'

He looked at me aghast. 'You're kidding,' he said. 'You have just got to be kidding.'

'Never more serious in my life. Let's go.'

In disgust he shrugged himself free. 'I'm going to find out what's happened.'

'No, Steve. I positively forbid it. We don't want to get mixed up in this.'

'But it could be your friend that's hurt.'

Steve pushed his way through the crowd, and spoke to the crewmember. He came slowly back. 'Your friend, Sir Eric, has been mugged, or something,' he said as if it were all my fault. 'He's being taken to hospital. He's unconscious.'

I was even more in a hurry to go. 'Yes, well, let's go, Steve.'

Steve shook his head in disbelief. 'I don't understand you, mate. Not at all.'

Then he saw the barman near the yacht looking at him thoughtfully. Suddenly the penny dropped, and Steve realised what the consequences might be if he got involved. He grabbed my arm. 'Come on mate,' he said. 'Time we was on the ferry and home.'

We half walked, half ran to the Customs Hall. There were few passengers waiting as yet, so we sat down and tried to look inconspicuous. Steve kept looking back to see if anybody was following, but we seemed to be in luck. Then Steve let out a groan. 'Shit,' he said.

'What's the matter? What is it?'

'The bloody barman. He's on to us.'

There was no escape. We were cornered. The barman came up to us looking very angry. 'You pay, señor,' he said to Steve. 'You owe me money.'

'You what?' Steve looked incredulous. Then his brow cleared. 'Oh yeah,' he said. He turned to me in relief. 'I forgot to tell you. I owe him money. I had a coffee, and didn't have no money.'

We fished out some money, and Steve tipped him lavishly. The man seemed well-satisfied and went happily back to his bar. Slowly the place filled up with other tourists, and eventually the boat revved up or whatever it does, and we swung out to sea. At last we could relax.

'What's going on?' Steve demanded.

'How should I know?' I replied. 'There are a lot of rough people in the drug business, and Sir Eric was in it up to his neck. I reckon he was getting out of Gibraltar for reasons we don't know about. Nothing to do with the market drying up as he claimed. On the other hand, it could be a simple mugging. He probably let the crew go ashore and was left on his own.'

Steve fell silent at that. We arrived back in Tangier much the worse for wear.

CHAPTER FOUR

MAGGIE

You could have knocked me down with a feather when Steve walked through the door last night. I was sitting in front of the telly, hoping he would phone me again, when I heard the key in the lock. I burst into tears, which seemed to please him.

'What's the matter with you then?' he grinned, hugging me tight.

All I could do was wail: 'Steve, Steve.'

He held me close, kissing me slowly and tenderly. He lifted me in his arms and carried me to bed. He made love to me that night so beautifully I could have forgiven him everything. He rolled over and lit a cigarette. 'So how was it?' I asked.

'The best,' he said grinning the while. 'You were great.'

'Not the sex, stupid. The trip.'

'Oh. The trip.'

'Well?'

He puffed away at his ciggie. 'It was hellish hot down there,' he said finally.

'Why are you back so early?'

'Not early. Never said it was going to be a long trip.' He was on the defensive again.

'Never said it would be so short, either,' I countered.

'Yes, well. ' He said nonchalantly. 'Jesus, I'm tired. It's been a long day. D'you mind if I go to sleep now? We'll talk in the morning.'

'Too damned right we will,' I muttered rebelliously. I could see it was no good continuing that night, but I was determined to get it out of him the next day. Whatever it was.

We woke early, and Steve went straight into the bathroom and the shower. I put on the kettle, wondering if I should lock the door somehow so that he couldn't leave the flat. He came out of the shower all wet and tousled looking very cheerful, sat down at the kitchen table and asked for orange juice.

'Orange juice?' I was amazed. 'You never have orange juice.'

'It's good for you,' he said. 'It gives you the right vitamins.'

'What do you know about vitamins?' I asked. 'You've never shown any interest in them before.'

'One never stops learning, does one?' he grinned.

'Are you feeling all right?' I asked.

'Never felt better.'

'Good,' I said, pouring him his tea. 'So now you can give me a complete version of your holiday.'

'Oh. Well.' He was looking sheepish again. 'Not much to tell.'

'Oh yes, there is,' I said firmly. 'Why are you back so early? And don't tell me it's not early, 'cos you've only been away a couple of days.'

He swallowed his tea. and passed his cup for a refill. 'Dickie wasn't too well. The heat you know.'

'No, I don't know, Steve. Stop prevaricating.'

'What's prevaricating?'

'That is. You're being evasive. Talk to me for God's sake.'

He sighed. 'Honest, Maggie, there's not much to tell. Honest. We was in an ever-so-nice hotel in Tangier, and we went to Gibraltar for the day. Dickie met a friend of his on a yacht -'

'A yacht? That's a bit posh, isn't it? Whose was it?'

'Er – can't remember. Some fat cat. I wasn't there long. Dickie was doing some business.'

'What kind of business?'

'How the hell should I know? I wasn't there at the time. I only came aboard after they'd finished.'

'Didn't you ask him?'

'Didn't seem polite. One has to mind one's manners.'

'What's all this "one" business? You're talking funny, Steve. I don't understand this at all.'

He considered this for a moment, then said, 'Any egg and sausage?'

I sighed and went to cook his breakfast. 'But I haven't finished with you yet,' I said. 'Just you wait.'

He grinned at me again; he really could be infuriating.

After he'd eaten, he lit a fag, and I went on the attack again.

'Well?' I began.

'Well what?'

'Stop hedging, Steve. Time to tell me everything.'

'I've told you, Maggie. Honest.' He was lying through his teeth. I could see that.

'So you go on holiday with an old poofter for a couple of weeks with no significant duties to perform. Just to look after him in some vague way. You stay a couple of nights in an "ever-so nice" hotel, go to Gibraltar, visit a yacht, then come home.'

'Right.'

'Come on Steve. Pull the other one. What are you up to? What's the old man's line of business?'

Steve blew out a cloud of smoke. 'Smuggling,' he said calmly.

'What?'

'Smuggling. He does a bit on the side. Only marijuana and that. Not the hard stuff.'

I was appalled. 'And you have to help him?'

'Not unless I want to. Which I don't, obviously.'

I was getting very scared. 'Steve,' I said, 'for God's sake, think what you're doing. You've been in trouble with the law once. If ever they catch you - '

'They won't,' he said confidently, ' 'cos I ain't doing nothing.'

'But you said -'

'I said the old boy's doing it. Not me. I've been given a clear choice, and I said no.'

'So you were approached?'

'I was asked, yes. And I refused.'

He looked so young and vulnerable and pleased with himself. He was the one who needed protecting – not me, or old Mr Grayson. 'Oh Steve -'

He put his arms round me and kissed my head. 'Don't worry, old girl,' he said. 'I can take care of meself.'

I doubted that – especially as he called me old girl. He's never called me that before.

'So, is that the end of it then? There are to be no more trips?'

'Er – no. He said he still wanted me – needed me – as he put it. He said he'd let me know. Meanwhile - ' he grinned triumphantly, 'I'm still being paid for doing nothing but sit on my ass and look at you.'

'Well, I've got to go to work, so you can get off your ass and do the shopping.'

'Better than that,' he grinned. 'We'll go out to dinner tonight. The first of many. Live it up a little.'

'We'll see about that,' I replied weakly, and left him to it.

All day I thought about him and his connection with this man. I could hardly concentrate on my work. I kept thinking of him getting into trouble with the police, and going to prison with a record. He said he wouldn't get involved – but did he mean it? Sometimes he looked so trusting and innocent it frightened me; other times he was playing the big butch he-man.

But in a relationship you've got to have trust, haven't you? I mean, without that there's nothing. I resolved to keep my thoughts to myself and enjoy the evening and him for as long as we had together.

When I got home that evening, he had the radio playing full blast (an annoying habit of his), and he was shaking with excitement. He picked me up and twirled me round that room.

'Whatever's the matter with you?' I said. Ever the wet blanket.

'Tonight we're going out on the town. We'll really have a night out together. Tomorrow. I've got to go up to London to get a visa.'

'Visa?'

'Yeah. We're leaving for India in a few days' time.'

STEVE

I was knackered by the time we got on the plane. Go to India House, Dickie said, and get a visa, he said. Sounds all right said like that. He never told me about the queues and form filling and waiting and that. And then I had to go back to collect the bloody thing the next day. By the time I had finished, I wasn't at all sure I wanted to go to India. I didn't even know why we was going to India. And knowing him, perhaps that was just as well. It was bound to be something dicey.

Anyway, I got back to Charing Cross, and caught the Ashford train – it was only the rush hour, wasn't it? I was hot and sticky and bad tempered by the time I got in the door, and what did I have to face? Another grilling from her, that's what. We got quite shirty with each other in the end, 'cos she just goes on and on. 'Why are you going?' 'Where are you going?' (India's a big place, and she wants specifics, don't she?) On and on and on she went. In the end I beat a dignified retreat into the bedroom; she follows on later looking a bit calmer like. I offer to take her out for a meal, but she says two nights running is spendthrift or something. Can't figure out women sometimes. They like to be treated like queens, but suddenly they get all holier than thou, and start on about wasting money – which isn't even theirs, is it? I'm earning good now with old Dickie, even if it's all a bit iffy.

Anyway, I got the bloody visa and that the next day, and goes out on a shopping spree to buy a few shirts and that. Dickie says I won't know what hit me heatwise, so I get meself a few nice T-shirts and a real nice pair of pants and shoes, and that. Get an earlier train this time, so on the way back home, I popped into the Paki newsagent on the corner and asked his advice like, on what to wear. Told me to buy it there – it'd be cheaper. Never thought of that. Too late now.

Then there was the vaccinations and all – and malaria tablets, which should have been started two weeks before we left, so they probably won't be any use either way. All this for a trip lasting eight days, Dickie said. So what with all the jabs and pills and that, I wasn't on top of meself when we left for Heathrow.

We was flying BA to Delhi in Business Class: quite a different kettle of fish from the old economy, I can tell you. Room to stretch your legs, food and drink and your own telly. No waiting about with the masses neither. You go to a special room for the nobs, where it's all quiet and peaceful like. So that bucked me up no end. I could get used to this life quite easy like.

All the same, it took forever to get there. Ten hours by my reckoning. We left late evening, and arrived next morning with six hours' time difference. Doesn't half play you up with your body clock, as Dickie said. We go to this Taj Mahal Hotel – although the Taj Mahal ain't in Delhi. All marble and air-conditioned, thank God. The hotel, that is, not the monument. If there was poverty in India, I had yet to see it.

I had been trying for days to find out why we was going to India but Dickie stayed stuum. I asked him about his pal Eric, but he said he knew nothing. Hadn't he tried to find out what had happened? Yes. So was it still smuggling he was up to, or what? No reply, except to tell me just to do my job. According to him, we was just doing a short tour of various places in

India; I was told to observe and absorb the culture. Travel broadens the mind, he said. I thought I was quite broad-minded enough, thank you all the same. Anyway, I was to watch what I ate or drank. And never touch the water, so when I went out to the hotel pool, I was almost scared to jump in. But I did: it was that hot and sticky. Everybody looked half dead with the heat. They was all waiting for the rains evidently. Must say we could do with a bit of rain to clear the air.

Of course I've heard of monsoons and that, but didn't know that rains was another name for it. ''Cos that's what happened the next day when we was going out on a coach tour of Delhi. We was with a sort of posh package tour, where you was looked after but could do what you liked – within reason, of course. We had this nice little Indian guide, Rana was her name. Tiny little thing, but ever so efficient. She thought nothing of lugging our cases in and out of the coach and being everyone's dogsbody. I felt quite sorry for her. Anyway, she'd got us all on board and organised for the Red Fort, when it started to rain. A few drops at first, and then it pelted down for the whole day. We was told it might go on for months like this. We had come in the monsoon season. Everyone knows that – except Dickie evidently. Christ, what a holiday this was going to be.

'Of course I knew about the monsoon.' he said irritably. 'This isn't the first time I've been here, you know.'

'Then why did we come now?' I persisted.

'It's convenient, that's why.' He was on the defensive, I could tell. Obviously he was up to his old tricks. So I asked him straight out.

'Come on, you should at least give me a clue, mate. What are we here for?'

But all he said was we should try and enjoy ourselves as much as we could. Only eight days. Make the most of it.

I could have been in England. There's enough rain there for my liking. I didn't need to travel all this way to watch it pissing down from morn to night.

RICHARD

Of course I'd tried to find out about Eric. Of course I had. He's my oldest friend, and I'm worried stiff. I rang the Annabella from Tangier before we left, but no one answered – not even a member of the crew. Gib hospital said he had been discharged that morning, but were disinclined to give me further information. I didn't dare ring the Gib Police. I rang his London number when we got back, but there was no reply. Odd that; usually there was a servant or answering machine or something. Just dead silence. His mobile was not answering either. I thought it best not to worry Steve too much. He has an odd sense of loyalty, that boy – commendable, but misdirected in this case.

He was thrilled I could tell about the India trip, but was disappointed to find the monsoon had already started. Nevertheless he was in good spirits when we sat down to dinner on our first night in Delhi. I spared him the spiced Indian diet on his first night, and took him up to the top floor of the hotel to the Casa Medici room, which had a Continental and Italian menu. He didn't expect beans and chips, thank goodness, and tucked into a pasta dish to the manner born. He is such a mixture of boyish charm, naiveté and that pseudo machismo which goes with earrings and tattoos. He asked me again about my plans: what we were supposed to be doing in India. He refused – unsurprisingly, given what had happened so far – to believe that we were here solely for pleasure. And yet that was the case – at least it was ninety-five per cent of the case.

He just kept grinning and shaking his head. 'Come on, Dickie old mate,' he wagged his finger at me, 'let me in on this. I deserve it.'

I side-tracked him by pretending to be outraged at his form of address.

'What should I call you then?' he demanded. He refused to call me Mr Grayson, and said Richard was far too stuffy. 'No, Dickie me lad, that's the best moniker for you. Suits you down to the ground.'

He looked me straight in the eye and grinned. I could feel my stomach turning to water. I waved to the wine waiter for another bottle.

Funny though. He didn't realise that the only person who had ever called me Dickie was my dear Philip. My mind went back to those days, and I drank deep to hide my tears. Dammit.

STEVE

My word he plays his cards close to his chest, does our Dickie. I can't get a thing out of him. He drives me nuts at times: he wants me to be open and honest with him all right, but not the other way round. Why he can't confide in me instead of landing me in it at the last moment, I'll never know. I suppose I'll get a sudden call for help when I least expect it.

There was a nice meeting with the rest of the group first, when we all got to know each other. Rana, our Indian guide, was ever so friendly and helpful and all. Then there was Mandy – with her mum – she was giving me the eye all right, but I had to eat with Dickie.

Anyway, we had a good nosh that first night in Delhi, with some food that wouldn't have disgraced our Italian trattoria at home. He was well into the wine as usual, and got quite tearful at one stage when I called him Dickie. He said someone else used to call him that way back. Poor old sod – you forget when they're old that they must've been young once themselves, and had a bit of nooky. Anyway, I tried to be understanding and that, and kept smiling sympathetically.

I asked him again about his mate, Eric, but got no joy. He looked shifty and fidgeted about. 'Don't you care?' It annoyed me that he didn't seem to be worried.

'Of course, I care,' he snapped back. 'What do you think I am? He's my oldest friend.'

'Then why -?'

'I've tried everything. I can't get hold of him. I don't know what's happened. So let's close the subject, shall we?' He was glaring at me now.

'OK, OK. Calm down.' I changed the subject and asked again what he was up to.

'What do you mean – up to?' He looked at me all innocence.

'Are you smuggling grass or what?'

'Certainly not,' he said indignantly. 'What do you take me for?'

'Dickie, come on now. Don't give me the goody-two-shoes crap. This is Steve you're talking to, remember? The guy who fished you out of trouble in Tangier, Gibraltar and all points south of the Channel.'

He smiled at that, and took a hefty swig of wine. 'I have no smuggling plans at the moment, Steve, I promise. I'm here on a shopping spree, that's all. Quite innocent, in fact.' He winked at me, which was a bad sign. I hadn't the nerve to ask what he was shopping for – I'd find out soon enough, that's for sure.

MAGGIE

He's gone again. He's off without a word. Well, that's not strictly true, but I could do with a wee bit more than a smile and a kiss on the cheek. Sometimes he's so offhand with me, and yet other times he's like the good old Steve I fell in love with. I wonder how long this is going to go on for.

Janet came round again last night. I know she means well, but I'm afraid she likes the bad news more than the good. And she's not exactly riding on the crest of the wave either from what she says. Andy's playing her up – at least that's what she claims. I'm not sure she's saying this to make me feel better or whether it's really true. Evidently he went down to the pub two nights ago and stayed till closing. She heard later that he was deep in conversation with a woman all night.

'So he's having it off with that besom,' Janet said, sloshing out the wine she'd brought. (Wine seems to be a necessity nowadays. I didn't used to drink much before.)

'You don't know that, Janet,' I tried to be comforting. 'It's all hearsay.'

'Hearsay, you say? Just wait till I catch hold of that slag. I'll give her hearsay.'

'What has Andy to say for himself?'

'Nothing. He never does. Men are all the same. They're all shites, so they are.'

I was inclined to agree with her. Ian was a bastard too. He was a bastard literally, but I meant how he had treated me. We were married when I was 19, all starry-eyed, marrying the sexiest hunk in Pilrig. I certainly got that wrong, didn't I? I was pregnant almost at once, and Ian wasn't at all impressed about that. When I was about six months gone, he started to go out nights, and leave me at home. He couldn't hold his drink either.

One night we had a row. My fault I suppose for criticising him when he was puggled, as we say, but I was fed up to here with his drinking and swearing. Anyway, he lost his rag and belted me one. That did it. From then on, the marriage was over. I tried to keep going until the baby was born, but even that wasn't to be. I had a miscarriage, and that was the end of that. I left Ian, and moved down south. Janet had married and moved to Ashford, so I stayed with them for a month or so till I found a place of my own.

I sighed. She wasn't making much sense, and I needed someone to talk sense that night. 'Well, anyway,' I began. 'Steve got off all right. He's away to India, you know.'

'I ken that fine,' she retorted.

'Wouldn't you like to go to India?'

'Course I would,' she spat scornfully. 'But not with an old poofter. A man'd do me fine.'

I had to agree with her. There's something very strange about Steve's friendship or whatever he likes to call it. What's the attraction? I'm sure Steve's not gay – or even bi. I'm sure I'd know.

Janet wanted us to have a night on the town – 'away from the shites' as she put it. I must say I was tired of sitting at home on my own every night, so we agreed to go out for a meal the next evening. After that, we sat together mostly in silence, each with our own thoughts. But we put away a bottle or two again.

It was becoming a habit.

STEVE

One thing about India is that it's hot. Wherever you are, whatever you do, you're in a muck sweat from the moment you stick your head out of your air-conditioned room. We was on our way to Agra to see this Taj Mahal thing everyone talks about. The coach tour the day before had been a washout, as it pissed down for the entire day, and we sat, miserable like in the coach, looking out at the poor buggers scavenging about in the rain. We certainly had a view of the poverty if nothing else.

The coach ride from Delhi to Agra wasn't all that long, but it wasn't half sticky. The air-conditioning broke down, and our guide, Rana, passed round iced drinks and smiles to keep our minds off the heat. It was still raining, but it was hot. The hotel was the Taj View – wherever you go it's Taj something or other- and no sooner did we arrive than we was hauled out again onto another coach to see the real Taj Mahal building.

When we got out of the coach, the rain stopped and the sun was coming out. We got to the entrance, which was more like a palace itself, and queued to go through the gate. Rana had given us a brief description of the place and what we would see, but said that once we was through the gate, she'd leave us alone, and wait for us to meet again in about an hour's time. I remembered the photo of poor Princess Diana sitting on a bench looking all sad and coy, but I wasn't prepared for what I saw when we stepped into the sunshine on the other side. There it stood – all cool and white against the deep blue sky. It looked as if it was taking off somehow – as if it was going to float through the air.

Dickie was looking at me waiting for a comment. I didn't know what to say; I didn't want to spoil it for want of the right words and that. I felt frustrated ''Cos I couldn't think of the right thing to say. I opened my mouth to say it was like Disneyland, but real and not fake, but thought 'don't put your foot in it this time'. So I said nothing like.

'Well, Steve, what do you think?' he prompted me for a reply.

'I dunno,' I muttered. 'It's good, innit?'

'Isn't it, Steve.' He had to correct me. 'Isn't it, not innit.'

'I know,' I said, and walked away from him.

It was like I was in a dream. I never knew a building could affect you like that, but as I walked nearer, and it got bigger, I felt excited and happy and exhilarated. I passed the bench where Di had sat; now there was dozens of tourists having their photos taken in the same spot, as if that meant anything, and I thought, what does anything matter?

'Nice, isn't it?' said this voice. I looked about and it was this girl who was on the tour with us. Name of Mandy – she was with her mum, but I saw she was interested in me.

'Yeah,' I replied, and walked on. I wasn't in the mood.

The hot sun was burning my head, but it felt good for once. I was really on a high, and wandered about like that for ages it seemed. There was a lot of people milling around, but it didn't make no difference. I was happy that's all. I took my shoes off and went inside and saw the tombs of the two lovers and that, and felt comfortable and content. It seemed right to have nothing on my feet, and feel the cool of the marble floor. I don't think I'd ever felt this kind of contentment before. It was great, I can tell you. I came out and thought, 'You know nothing, Steve, my lad, nothing at all. But that's all right, 'cos nobody else knows nothing neither. Either'. On the way back to the gate, I went through the gardens full of trees, all green and peaceful like. Nobody went off the main path it seemed, so I was alone apart from a couple of gardeners, who smiled and waved as I passed. Those gardens was restful too.

'My God, look at me,' I said to meself. I was feeling real uplifted. I met up with Dickie at the gate. They was all waiting for me, and Dickie was watching me worried like.

I looked at him. 'Cheers, mate,' was all I could say.

We got into the coach and went back to the hotel.

RICHARD

Steve was very quiet that evening over dinner. I couldn't quite determine whether he had enjoyed The Mausoleum or not. He'd left me abruptly at the entrance, and gone off on his own. I thought it best to leave him to his own devices. But when he came back, he had looked so strange: almost as if he'd had some kind of religious experience. But that couldn't be – a man like that. So conversation was very perfunctory at dinner until we had finished the pudding, when he looked at me and said: 'Tell me about this here Hinduism and that.'

My mouth dropped wide open. 'What do you want to know exactly?'

'Well,' he replied, 'I was talking to Rana at the desk like, when I was sending me postcards. And she said there was all sorts of gods here in India right. Elephants like Ganesh and that. She said that Christians and that were in the minority.'

'That's true indeed. There are comparatively very few Christians in India. Actually, I'm not quite sure of the percentage, but Christianity isn't the predominant religion in the world.' I followed this with a brief lecture on the various world religions, and to my surprise, Steve listened to me with interest.

'So,' he asked when I had finished, 'there's a sort of battle like between the Hindus, Buddhists, and Muslims?'

'Not a battle exactly, but that was the reason Pakistan was created – to separate the Muslim community.'

He went quiet after that: surely the boy wasn't getting religion?

MAGGIE

We didn't have our night out after all. The next day my washing machine packed up, and I spent the whole morning trying to find someone to come and see to it. Eventually this friend of Janet's, well not a friend exactly, but someone who had fixed her machine a few months ago, came to look at it. The kitchen floor was soaked, as the machine had done its nut in the middle of the night, and when I came in the next morning, I was swishing about in dirty water. Cleaning it up hadn't left me in the best of tempers. Eventually this guy, Alan, came round. He turned out to be Scots too, from Glasgow, though, not Edinburgh. He gave me a pretty gloomy prognosis: it wasn't a simple fuse, but the microchip or whatever had blown and had to be replaced. He told me how much it would cost.

I felt like crying. Why does everything go wrong at once? Steve away, then a packed-up washing machine seemed to be the last straw. I made him some tea, and we got to chatting. I stupidly told him about Steve, and how I missed him and everything. He was sympathetic, and told me how his live-in partner had upped and left him last week. So we were two poor wee abandoned weans. This made me feel worse, not better, and my eyes filled with tears again. I wanted Steve back so much.

'Come on, it's not so bad,' he said, misunderstanding. 'I'll away round to the store and get the spare part. I'll be back this afternoon, and it'll be up and running for you this evening.'

He was as good as his word. He didn't get back till nearly five, though, so I had to stay in all afternoon waiting. Anyway he fixed it, and offered to give me a reduction if I didn't want a receipt. It saved VAT for him, and fifteen or so off for me, so we were both happy.

I showed him to the door, but he hesitated a bit. 'I suppose you wouldn't come out with me sometime?' he asked. 'Just for the company.'

'No, I couldn't, possibly,' I blurted out before I had a chance to think. He smiled. He was quite the opposite of Steve: smallish, wavy black hair, fantastic white teeth like a film star's; maybe they were false.

'No, course not,' he said, and smiled again. 'See yous around.' And with that he was gone.

I sat down and regretted the missed opportunity. After all, what was wrong with going out with a guy for a drink or whatever? The whatever bit, that's what. One thing leads to another, doesn't it, and before you know it, you've got yourself in a jam.

Pity though. He was a nice guy. Gentle, I could tell.

STEVE

The next day we was supposed to be going to the Agra Fort in the afternoon, but the morning was free for shopping with the group or on your own, so Dickie said I could do what I liked. I didn't feel like another look at the Taj Mahal, or just sitting by the pool by meself, so I asked him what he was up to.

'Nothing much, me lad,' he twinkled. 'Doing a bit of shopping, that's all.'

'Oh yeah? What kind of shopping?'

'Perfectly legitimate, I can assure you,' He was all excited and anxious to be gone.

'Can I come with you then?' I asked.

He looked surprised. 'Why yes, of course, Steve. If you really want to. I thought you'd like some time to yourself.'

'Nah,' I said. 'I'd better keep an eye on you. Better for both of us.'

He laughed at that. 'Come on then. I'll show you how to make some money without even trying.'

We left the hotel together, crossed the road and walked down a bit. There was a lot of shops and emporiums, as they call them, but Dickie knew where he was going. We turned into this doorway, and down the stairs, past carpets and all kinds of stuff. At the bottom was this big room like, with all kinds of marble tables and that.

Dickie knew what he was doing all right, and asked for some man with a foreign Indian name, Ganesh Ram I think it was, Ganesh being the, elephant god. He was greeted by this guy enthusiastically, and tea was produced and drank. Dickie sat like some king surrounded by his minions as they produced all these marble tables. I must say I've never seen anything like them – the marble was so pure and they had inlaid semi-precious stones. Dickie told me all about it after. He knew what to look for: you have to be sure first of all that it is marble and not alabaster. Then what kind of stones they are. The elephant man brought in this beautiful table, and put a light underneath. It was so transparent, the table glowed all pinky-white. Translucent, Dickie called it afterwards.

After a lot of haggling and shaking of heads, Dickie bought two. I must say they would go down a treat in Ashford. He paid by credit card, and arranged to have them shipped over, at a giveaway price.

He wasn't half pleased with himself as we came out. 'What do you think, Steve? Like them?'

I had to admit they was great. 'What's the point in buying two?' I asked.

'Investment, Steve, investment. When we get back to England, I'll sell them for more than twice the price. And that'll more or less pay for our holiday. How about that?'

You gotta admire the old geezer, you really do. No flies on him and no mistake.

MAGGIE

We had our night out eventually. And it turned into a real hen party. Janet met a couple of her mates in the pub, and we all set off on a pub-crawl in Ashford – not the most exciting place in the world. Ashford isn't Glasgow or Edinburgh. Finally we landed up in a disco, by which time I was in need of my bed, when who should come on the scene but Alan of the washing machine.

'How's it going?' he asked.

'Oh fine,' I had to shout in the din. 'I got all my washing done fine.'

He laughed at that. 'I didnae mean the washing machine, hen,' he laughed. 'I was talking about you.'

'Oh,' I said. 'All right, I suppose. The same. And you?'

'Likewise. Wanna dance?'

'No thanks. I was just going home. I'm a wee bit tired.'

'Me too,' he said. 'I'll walk you home.'

'There's no need,' I protested, though I must say it's better to be walking the streets with a laddie than alone. 'Come on,' he said.

We said goodnight to the girls, who were all cackling and nudging each other. What you have to put up with.

The streets were fairly quiet, and we got home fairly quickly. I felt I'd better ask him up for a cuppa or something. 'That'd be great,' he said.

We climbed the stairs in silence, and I went into the kitchen to put the kettle on. This was one big mistake, and I knew it. I could feel him coming up behind me. His arm went round my waist. 'Maggie,' he said softly.

I knew it. I knew it. It was bound to happen, wasn't it? What I needed most in the world that minute was a man's arms around me. And there he was. Not Steve, but Alan. 'Alan, don't.' I said half-heartedly.

His hand stayed where it was, and he turned me round to face him. 'You mean that?'

'Yes.'

'Really?'

'Alan, I've still got Steve. He's away, that's all. I – '

He kissed me softly on the mouth, and his arm tightened round me.

I knew then I was a goner.

I felt dirty and guilty afterwards of course. I'd cheated on Steve, and when you do that, it's usually the beginning of the end. He wanted to stay the night, but I hustled him out of the flat as quick as I could. He wants to see me again, but I don't know. Life has to go on with or without Steve: it's just I don't know where I stand with him.

Of course I haven't heard from him – and I hardly expected to, with India being so far away. Phoning would be expensive, and their time is all wrong compared with ours. Still, I'm in a mess. Janet rang the next day to find out what had happened. She, of course, was as pleased as punch. 'Go for it,' she urged me. 'You only live once.'

That's all very well, but where do I stand with Steve? I wish he'd come back home, and we can sort this out.

STEVE

And so his shopping spree went on and on. A carpet here, woodwork there. Silk by the yard and everything. His credit cards must be taking a bashing, but as he says, he'll recoup the lot and more when we get back.

I must say I really like this place. India's not at all what I expected. Sure there's the poverty and that, but it has a richness about it. Religion seems to dominate everything, but that's all right. Their religion fits in here, more than ours does in England, I reckon. At least it seems so to me.

We did a quick trip to the Agra Fort in the afternoon, and Rana was in her element lecturing us on what it was all about. I'd never really registered her before as a bit of skirt, probably because she was always wearing a sari, but she was some dolly bird all right when you weighed her up. She was tiny, and a lovely golden brown colour with the reddest lips and whitest teeth. Her black hair was long and hung down to her shoulders. I wasn't sure if she was giving me the eye like, but when she was showing us the view of the Taj Mahal across the river, her hand touched my arm. Not sure if it was accidental or what. I caught Dickie's watching me with a funny look on his face. I wasn't sure whether he approved or not.

We left on the coach the next morning and seen some fantastic palace miles from anywhere, and then had lunch. After a long drive (thank God the airconditioning was mended), we arrived in Jaipur. And this hotel was something else. It had been palace too; Rambagh Palace it was called, and it sure was a palace. We was both tired that night and went to bed early. I began to think of Rana, and then of Maggie, and how I'd left her. I wasn't very proud of meself for that, but you've got to take your opportunities, haven't you? I'd probably never have seen this lot if I hadn't come with Dickie, but I wish she could have come too. I lay in bed with my face in the pillow, and I could almost smell her sweet hair. The old groins stirred as they say, and that put an end to sleep for some time.

Next morning we was up nice and early to go to the Palace of Winds. Dickie phoned from his room to say he'd been sick – eating too much as usual, I expect. But not to worry, nothing serious, I was to go ahead and enjoy meself. So I went down for breakfast and then onto the coach. Strange, I felt funny without Dickie, you'd think I'd be happy to be off the leash. And that Mandy girl was sitting across the aisle with her mother, leering at me like some old tart. This Palace of the Winds turned out to be a pink building in the middle of the city. In fact the whole city was pink, and the people was dressed in red and other vivid colours. We all got out of the coach to look at it from across the road, and people was taking photos and that. I was just looking and trying to understand what Rana was saying, when she gave a shriek and pulled me towards her.

There was this snake charmer (they're all over the place in India) sitting cross-legged on the pavement, piping up his cobra. It had done its usual weaving about and was starting to focus on me legs. I was in me shorts at the time. I was scare shitless, I can tell you. Everyone screamed, then laughed, then took more photos and that. The natives didn't bat an eyelid. Rana said there wasn't any real danger as the snakes were all neutered or whatever you do to snakes. Still, they're evil-looking bastards at the best of times, and I was glad to get on the coach again. When I looked out of the window, the snake charmer was packing up his cobras to take a breather until the next coachload.

Then we went on to this Amber Fort. That turned out to be something too. After about half an hour's drive up the hills, we got out and found we had to queue to go up the hill on an elephant. It was hot queuing in the sun, but eventually I was hanging on to this howdah thing, trying to balance meself on top of this elephant. Last time I'd done that was at the zoo when I was a kid, but this was the real thing. Rana was sitting next to me and laughed as I wobbled about when the bloody animal started to move.

'You'll soon get used to it,' she said.

Elephants are not the fastest animals in the world, and the journey up the winding hill seemed like forever. The slow majestic lurching back and forth was making me drowsy too. I tried to explain this to Rana, who called it soporific. She knows English better than me. The slow movement to and fro was also affecting me lower parts, especially when I looked at her. The sari she was wearing that day was very dark blue, yet very thin material, as if you could see right through it. You couldn't of course, but it looked like it. She kept smiling at me too. I still wasn't sure whether this was a come-on, or she was just being polite to one of her group. Anyway I smiled a lot back, and felt meself getting the biggest hard-on I'd had for months. God it was hot.

When we got to the top, she busied herself with organising us all. I couldn't take my eyes off her all morning, and on the way back in the coach when she was dishing out the cold bottled water, our fingers touched briefly. And our eyes met, too. God, where was this leading? I thought of Maggie, and how I felt last night, and she seemed a million miles away. It started to rain buckets again.

The usual carpet shop stop was made, and then back to the hotel for something to eat. I went up to see Dickie, who was looking a bit white. A trip to the City Palace and Observatory was planned for the afternoon, but Dickie said he'd rather stay in. I could do what I liked. Normally I wouldn't have bothered with the tour, but little Rana was fascinating me more and more. So off I went in the coach again.

It had cleared up at lunch, but as soon as we got in the coach, it pelted down again. As the Observatory turned out to be in the open air, we all decided to give it a miss. Looked pretty primitive to me anyhow. The City Palace was impressive all right; all these places are. I was itching to get nearer Rana, but she was playing hard to get, or at least giving that impression. She spent the afternoon explaining to the others or answering their questions or generally being efficient. I just felt frustrated – even humiliated like. The afternoon passed slowly, making me ever so frustrated and irritable.

On our return to the hotel, there was no sign of Dickie, so I got me bathing things, and set off for the pool, which was in the grounds. That was a fantastic place: a huge indoor pool, dark and mysterious, with water the colour of emeralds. I was all on my own. I dived into this still green water and felt like some god or other. It was just great. I'd done a couple of lengths, and they were lengths – the pool seemed miles long – when I saw a figure watching me from the other end. It was Rana.

My pulse started to race – just when I'd calmed meself down too, and was thinking nice pure thoughts and all. As I swam up to her end, she just stood there, and smiled. God, she was a knockout. I pulled meself up and out of the water.

'Hi,' I said, trying to control my breathing and other things.

'Hello, Mr Jackman,' she said. 'You swim well.'

'Thanks,' I replied. 'You having a dip?'

'No. I just came to remind you we are leaving early tomorrow afternoon. I should have told you on the coach, but I forgot. So sorry.'

'That's all right. It's nice to see you. And chat with you alone like.'

She smiled, and turned to go.

'Fancy a drink or something?' I asked her quickly. 'Tea, or something stronger?'

'Tea would be nice,' she said. 'But I really haven't time. I've promised to take some of the group shopping. You're welcome to come if you like.' Again the sweet smile. I thanked her for the offer, but shopping with the rest of the gang wasn't what I had in mind. As she turned, I caught hold of her arm, and pulled her toward me.

'You're all wet,' she said, hardly in protest.

'Yeah,' I said, hungry to get my tongue in her mouth. She smelled of India too, a strange spicy perfume, don't know what. She didn't resist, but didn't encourage neither. I kissed her gently at first, not wanting to frighten her. Her mouth stayed closed. I tapped my tongue gently on her lips, and after what seemed eternity, the gates opened and I was in.

A banging door, and voices, American voices, sounded. We was no longer alone. She pulled away, and with a quick smile was gone.

'Shit,' I said to meself. I dived into the pool again to cool off and get away from the people who were crowding in. I didn't feel like a god no more, just a poor sap from England. It wasn't till I got back to my room again that I wondered how she knew I was in the pool in the first place.

RICHARD

I mustn't be jealous. I mustn't be jealous. It's silly, but I am. I can feel that familiar gnawing at my stomach. Of course, he's attracted to that Rana girl. Of course he is. She's a very beautiful child. Too young for him, of course – Oh God, stop this. Don't say it, don't admit to yourself that you've fallen in love with him. I watched him watching her, eyeing her, waiting to have a word with her. Now I just lie in my room letting my imagination work overtime. What are they doing? Where are they now?

Yet I have his best interests at heart. I really do. I am a very foolish, fond old man, as Shakespeare says. I felt a little better about lunchtime, so I thought I'd pop down and have a stroll through the gardens. It had been raining, but it had cleared up and it was pleasant in the shade of the trees and bushes. I sat on a bench for a while, and perhaps I dozed off. Later, in the distance, I saw them returning from their tour, and hastened back to meet Steve, but by the time I reached the veranda, he had gone. I sat there a while, trying to calm my thoughts; time lies heavy away from your love. Then I saw him making for the pool by the bushes. I half got up to follow him, when I saw Rana walking towards me, smiling sweetly, to ask how I was. She wanted to tell me the plans for tomorrow – our last day. I knew we were free to go shopping in the morning, and then get the coach back to Delhi at 2 p.m. Rana had organised a shopping tour for the morning and wanted to know if I would be joining them. I declined gracefully, as I had my own plans for our last day. She also wanted to tell Steve: 'Shall I speak to your companion or will you?'

'I will,' I said too quickly. Then I realised how it must have sounded. 'Funny word to choose, companion, isn't it?'

'Well, I wasn't sure at first,' she replied. 'I thought he was your son, until I checked my list. You have different names.'

'He's not my son,' I said. 'I wish he were.'

When I said that, I realised that was exactly what I wished. My feelings for Steve were ambiguous without doubt, and, old as I am, I found his sexual attraction almost overwhelming. But I also felt something else – something much deeper. Yes, I wished he were my son.

I looked at her and smiled. 'Why not see him yourself?' I said. 'I think he's gone for a swim.'

She thanked me gravely, smiled her sweet smile, and made for the pool.

I got out of my chair, and stretched myself. I felt very old and useless. Perhaps I should have a nap before attempting some food later in the evening. I made my way upstairs to bed.

STEVE

Dickie had something to eat in his room that night; he said he was feeling much better, and tomorrow we would be going shopping in the morning before catching the coach, so I was to pack my bag before we left. I had dinner with Rana – and another five in the group – so there was nothing doing in that department, although Mandy was panting away. I think that one's a nympho or something. Or may be she's just as repressed and frustrated as me. We all want the one who don't want us, ain't it the truth? Anyway, I went to bed on me own, feeling real down and that. Didn't sleep well, neither.

I rang him next morning, and he sounded quite chirpy. Said we was to meet in the lobby in half an hour. So I went down as ordered at the right time, and saw him coming our of the safe deposit place with a large manila envelope. He took me into a corner. 'See this packet, Steve?' he said quiet like, 'Well, it's got thousands of dollars in it. We're about to make the purchase of the century.'

'Whad'ya mean?' My mouth was hanging open at the sight of all that money.

'We're going shopping for gems,' he explained,' and rubies in particular. A Burma Star with a bit of luck. Payment in foreign cash is often required, and anyway you get a better price for them this way. Here,' he handed me the packet,' you take care of the money. And don't lose it for God's sake.'

Suddenly the holiday was over and responsibility was on me. This is what I had been employed for. It took me a while to adjust.

Dickie had sailed out of the hotel and had the man call a taxi. In we was bundled and Dickie told him to take us to Johari Bazar.

'You know where we're going then?' I asked, clutching the packet in my sticky hands. I'd got no pockets big enough. He should have warned me.

'Eric gave me this address ages ago,' he replied. 'One can get a good bargain if one knows what one's doing.'

'And do you?' I corrected meself.' Does one?' That didn't sound right neither.

'You'd be surprised at my talents, Steve my boy,' he laughed. 'Actually,

I know quite a bit about gems.'

The taxi screeched to a halt and the usual arguments went on about the fare as the driver hadn't started the meter. Dickie disdainfully sorted that out and looked about him. 'The factory's up here somewhere,' he said.

We was at the gates of the Pink City, as they call the old part of town. It's the right name for it all right. The walls and buildings is all painted in this pink colour, and in the sun it looks real great against the blue sky. The traffic was indescribable – nothing in Europe could compare to this chaos. The noise was deafening, but Dickie sailed on oblivious.

'Ah, here we are,' he said turning up a side street by the LMB Hotel and into a small, scruffy-looking shop. 'Now, all I want you to do is look strong and tough. Keep quiet, hold on to the money and agree with whatever I say.'

In we went.

We was met by a small, skinny Indian in a dirty red turban, and a boy assistant with a squint. It all looked distinctly dodgy to me.

'Are you Krishna Rao?' asked Dickie imperiously.

The man looked at him suspiciously. 'How you know that name?' he asked.

'My great friend, Sir Eric Davies recommended you and your factory to me.' Dickie introduced himself (but not me), and at the mention of Eric's name, the man fell over himself with the fawning act. Dickie had called this place a factory, and at first I thought he had made a mistake. But now I could see the front was just the selling area, and through the door at the back was sounds of great activity. They really were cutting the stones and that. We was taken on a tour of the 'factory'. A grotty-looking place if ever I saw one. The unions would have something to say about their working conditions if it was in the UK. Most of the 'workers' were no more than kids, poor little blighters, working as if their lives depended on it. Probably did.

Krishna showed us how the gems was cut and polished: some of the machinery looked very much a hit or miss affair, but they was producing the goods all right. I saw some diamonds being polished on what they call a 'dop stick' – a kind of stick with the stone stuck on the end of it, the grinding wheel cutting as it went. Looked a bit primitive to me. But the really good stones were being cut proper on a cutting machine. It was quite interesting actually.

We was conducted back to the shop area, and tea was brought out and drank. Even I was treated to a cup. I have to admire Dickie in these situations. He behaves quite differently from the loveable old faggot I had got to know. Here was the stern English sahib, who knew everything and stood no nonsense. He asked to see emeralds first, not rubies.

After tea, Krishna went back into the factory, and came back with a tray of small stones, all green. Emeralds. I'd never seen gems like this before, and at the mention of the prices in dollars, which I could just about convert into pounds, my stomach turned to water. I prayed he knew what he was doing.

I relaxed a little when he produced from his pocket one of them jeweller's eyeglasses. (Later Dickie told me it was called a loupe, which is stronger than the ordinary eyeglass, and in fact he was only using it to impress the bloke. Anyone with half an eye can judge the quality according to Dickie.) Dickie frowned. 'No,' he said, shaking his head, 'I don't think so. They're too watery – there are too many inclusions in these.'

Krishna Rao was impressed, and disappeared to get another tray.

'Ah,' said Dickie at once. 'These look a little better.' And proceeded to examine them through his loupe, discarding them one by one.

'This is extremely light and slight greyish. No, no. I'm looking for a really good specimen.'

'If you come back tomorrow morning, Sahib,' Krishna Rao fawned, 'I'll have some new stones we are in the process of cutting now.'

'Not possible, I'm afraid,' said Dickie, rising to go. 'We leave early this afternoon.'

Krishna expressed regret and spoke rapidly to the boy in Hindi. The boy scuttled away and reappeared with a smaller tray, this time with only three stones on it. 'Ah,' said Dickie at once. 'Ah, that's more like it.' He picked up the largest stone and held it in his hand. I knew nothing about emeralds, but to me it was just fantastic: dark green, yet clear and mysterious – just like the water in the swimming pool. I thought of that cavernous place and Rana.

Dickie examined it thoroughly with his loupe and then through something called a Chelsea Filter, then he took it to the window.

'Facing north?' he asked.

Krishna nodded. 'Good.' He held the emerald up to the natural light, then grunted and turned to me. 'What do you think, Steven?' he asked, as if I was an expert.

His back was to Krishna, and he gave me a wink.

'Well,' I said as if considering, 'depends on the price, don't it?'

'You're right, Steven, it does indeed.'

The haggling began and went on for some time. They seemed to come to a dead end. 'What about rubies?' asked Dickie suddenly, as if it was an afterthought. 'Got any good rubies?' And the whole thing started all over.

Out came a tray of rubies, this time top-quality. Krishna wasn't going to muck about. Dickie went through his loupe performance again. Finally he was shown a beautifully clear dark red stone. Dickie squinted at it closely.

'Could be synthetic,' he pronounced.

'No, no sir, not synthetic. Proper Burma Star ruby. All are real true gems in this shop.'

'I must say it's the finest red I've seen yet,' Dickie muttered and took it to the window. He looked at it for some time. (Dickie explained it all to me on the plane going home. He was looking for the rays of asterism – a six-rayed star can be seen in the interior of a Burma Star ruby. He told me that save one leg, which was slightly weak towards the end, all the rays were straight and strong. I wish I could do something like that, but you'd need a lot of schooling I expect.) Anyway, his nibs announced that it was the genuine article, while Krishna nodded, trying to look hurt at his honesty being questioned.

Dickie then asked to see some diamonds. This part of the business didn't take so long. Krishna produced a tray of white diamonds cut and polished. Dickie inspected them and chose a couple of five carat stones. People say that diamonds is cold and hard, but to me their brilliance was like the sun blazing onto pure ice

Dickie hummed and hawed for a while, then finally made an offer: 'Tell you what. Give me a quote for the whole package. – the emerald, the ruby and the two diamonds.'

This time Krishna huffed and puffed. It was very tiring all this haggling – I don't know where Dickie gets his stamina from. Yesterday he was sick, yet here he was fresh as a daisy, and looked as if he could stay that way for hours.

In the end, he won. Unusual I'd imagine for someone to beat down an Indian, but he wore down Krishna, who ordered the boy to go out to his fridge for some mineral water. After what seemed ages, the boy returned balancing three glasses and two bottles of cold water on a tray. He managed to put the tray on the desk all right, but knocked over a glass, which shattered on the floor. Krishna swore at him loudly and gave him one on the ear hole. They both disappeared under the desk to pick up the pieces.

'So sorry. So sorry,' mumbled Krishna, hitting the boy again, who ran into the back room in tears. I felt quite sorry for him, poor little mite.

Anyway, we all had a swig of lovely cold water, and things calmed down a bit. Krishna sat down behind the desk: he was quite short so he looked a bit silly with the desk coming up to his chest like. The emerald was first wrapped in a piece of chamois and then in a gem paper, which is a small square of ordinary paper with two layers of a sort of wax paper to protect them from scratching and that. The ruby was placed in a separate gem paper, and finally the two diamonds were laid side by side in a third gem paper. Then they was folded over and over until they became a kind of tiny envelope. The three envelopes lay side by side on the table, and Krishna then turned to Dickie with a smile.

Dickie nodded and put his hand out to me for the money. I handed it over, and Dickie counted it out aloud so that we all could hear. Krishna nodded, satisfied and whistled for the boy. He came back and took the money, while Krishna picked up the three tiny envelopes and asked if Dickie wanted them in a packet.

'No, thanks,' said Dickie. 'I'll take them as they are.'

'Wouldn't you like a receipt?' asked the trader.

'No,' said Dickie, but then changed his mind. 'Well, maybe it would be wise, in case there's any difficulty in England.'

The trader rummaged about in the cluttered drawer of the desk for his receipt book. He had to practically empty the drawer on top of the desk before he found it. Eventually he found it and signed the slip with a flourish, and handed it to Dickie together with the gems. More tea was offered, but Dickie got up and said we must be on our way. With lots of hand shaking and smiles and that, we left the shop.

Dickie was triumphant. 'We've done well there, Steve. That ruby's a real beauty, and very valuable. To say nothing of the emerald and diamonds. They'll fetch twice that price in London.'

I was chuffed he included me in the deal as if I'd done anything. He gestured imperiously for a taxi: amazingly one stopped and we got in. I gave the address of the hotel, and we weaved through the dense traffic. Suddenly Dickie shouted to the driver. 'Just a minute, young man,' he cried, fishing out a dirty piece of paper from this pocket. 'Take us instead to Mirza Ismael Road – the Gem Testing Laboratory.'

That needed some elaboration as it wasn't on the Ismael Road at all, but the guy understood eventually. 'We might as well have the gems valued and tested by the experts,' Dickie explained. He settled back in the old banger and hummed all the way to the Lab, which, in fact, took about a minute it was so near. It'd have been quicker to walk.

There was a sour-faced girl behind the desk thing, who told us to come back that afternoon. I put on me charm act, telling her we was leaving in a few hours and couldn't she just oblige us seeing as how? Dickie was watching me with a strange look, half admiring and half disapproving. But was happy enough when she agreed. Dickie paid her the fee, and we hung about waiting.

She finally came back with the report. As Dickie had thought, the emerald and diamonds were good stones and would fetch a good price in London. Then his face went white. 'Jesus,' he said, showing me the report. 'The ruby – it's worthless. It's synthetic and not a very good one at that.'

I couldn't believe it – Dickie had been so sure, and seemed to know such a lot about it. I didn't know what to say.

'Let me look at that bloody stone,' he cried, tearing off the wrapping. He fumbled for his loupe, but it only need one look for him to know. 'Steve,' he shouted, This isn't the same stone. It isn't the one I bought. We've been had.'

Even I could see the difference. Once you've seen the real thing you can't mistake it, not really. 'It's not possible, it's not possible,' Dickie was shouting.

Then I realised what had happened. 'He must have switched packets when he was fiddling about in the drawer for that receipt book,' I said.

'But how did he know to have a ruby there?'

'The boy, remember? When the boy came back with the tray of mineral water and that, he must have brought in another gem paper with the fake ruby. There was a kerfuffle when he broke the glass, remember? Old Krishna must have palmed it then. They was speaking in Hindi all the time, so we didn't know what they was saying.'

Poor Dickie was getting hysterical, shouting and waving the report up and down. The girl asked him where he'd bought the stones, but she couldn't identify the address he gave her. 'Krishna Rao died years ago,' she said. 'I don't know who has that place now. Not reputable at all.' She shook her head. 'You should have gone to the Gem Palace,' she said. 'You need to buy from reputable people.'

He didn't need a lecture at that stage: 'What shall I do?' he wailed.

'Better go to the Police,' she advised.

'Police?' he shouted. 'Fat lot of good that'll do in this country. They'll not arrive till tomorrow morning, if that.'

This wasn't helpful at all; it was time for me to take charge. 'Come on Dickie, let's go,' I said, pushing him forcibly out into the street.

'I'll have to go back to the shop,' he panted. 'You try and get the police or something.'

'No, Dickie, my lad,' I said firmly. 'This is what you hired me for, and this is what we're going to do. You get a taxi back to the hotel, find Rana, get her to call the police or whatever, and then bring her to the shop. We may need someone who can talk the lingo.'

He could see the sense in that, but still hesitated: 'Are you sure you know what to do, Steve?' He asked plaintively.

'Yes,' I said, sounding tougher than I felt. 'Go.'

I whistled down a taxi, another minor miracle, and pushed him inside. Off he sped, and I screwed meself up to do the hero act. I'd sounded confident enough, but hadn't a clue what to do. There was no more taxis about, but plenty of rickshaws. I figured I could run faster than them, so I took off like a bat out of hell. I raced through the crowded streets, banging into people, pushing them aside, not saying sorry or nothing. I knew the shop was near, but with the crowds and that, it was difficult to work it out. It was getting real hot, and the sun was beating down on the old pink city. It would have looked great if I'd had the time to appreciate it. I hoped I'd find the shop again 'cos I had no idea of the address. Then I remembered it was by the LMB Hotel. I asked a few people, but all I got was 'buy my packet' or 'come to my gem factory'. It seemed the whole of Jaipur was selling gems and that, but nobody would give me a simple direction.

At last I saw the hotel. It had been so near all the time. I turned into the alley, and burst into the shop.

Krishna Rao was still there tidying up his desk. The boy was nowhere to be seen. He looked at me surprised. 'Closed,' he said.

'I don't think so,' I replied.

'What you want? We're closed,' he repeated.

'All I want, Krishna me lad, is the ruby we bought. Just give me the right packet and I'll be on my way.'

'What you mean?' He was looking a bit scared now. He obviously thought we wouldn't notice the swap till much later when we was gone.

'You switched the packet. We bought a Burma Star, and you gave us synthetic crap.'

'No, sir. You got what you paid for.'

'Listen Krishna, me lad,' I took him by the neck and pushed him down onto the desk. 'I'm in no mood to argue. Either you give me the bloody ruby, or I squeeze the life out of you right now. Understood?'

The man started screaming and jabbered away in Hindi. I was wondering what the hell I should do next, when there was a shout from the factory and two guys burst in. Right villains they looked too. They was all babbling away in Hindi, another disadvantage as far as I was concerned. These friends of Krishna's was looking murderous: I thought they might have knives or something.

Best thing was to hold Krishna as a kind of shield. I picked him up off the desk. He was surprisingly light – couldn't be eating many square meals a day, poor sod. While I was at it, I picked up a couple of packets from the desk and shoved them in my pocket. 'Come on, Krishna,' I glared at him. 'We're going walkies.'

The two men was taken aback by this tactic, and shouted more Hindi at Krishna, who was in no position to reply. 'Out the way you bastards,' I shouted, and pushed past them. I managed to gset into the alley, where a few people scuttled by. I set Krishna down on his feet, while the men came out of the shop behind me and screamed and threatened, but didn't touch me.

'Piss off, you two,' I shouted, and turned to some more Indians gathering round. 'Take me to the British Consul.' People is always saying this in films, aren't they, but I don't really know what for, or what he does when you get there. Anyway, it had some effect, because a path was cleared, and I got to the street by the LMB Hotel still holding on to Krishna.

People was yelling and screaming and little Krishna Rao was struggling away, and I didn't know what to do next. Then on the other side of the street to my amazement, I saw Rana coming out of a jeweller's shop with some of our group. I'd forgotten she said she was taking them shopping. I shouted to her. They saw me and waved. Mandy was there too, all smiles and 'hello, what are you doing here?'

I quickly explained to Rana, who took things firmly in hand. We trouped into the LMB and she phoned the police, telling Krishna to knock it off in Hindi. The police arrived surprisingly quick, and took charge of Krishna. I explained what had happened. We all went back to the shop and Krishna was forced to give me the packet with the real ruby.

I must say the Police wasn't very sympathetic: they seemed to think it was all our fault for being so stupid. Even Rana was surprised to hear we had been conned. 'The oldest trick in the world,' she said. Anyway, I'd managed to phone Dickie and set his mind at rest, and was glad when we was allowed to go. I said we wouldn't be pressing charges, but the Police didn't seem to understand what I meant. People is always saying that in England, you hear it on the telly all the time.

I got meself a taxi and went back to the hotel and left the group to their shopping. Dickie was in his room, but had left a message at the desk for me to go up. I knocked on his door, and his face, white as death, peered out at me.

'Are you all right, Steve?' he asked anxiously.

'Never better, mate,' I said breezily. 'Here's your ruby.' Dickie examined it quickly and sighed with relief. 'God, Steve, you're a wonder. I don't know how to thank you.'

'It's me job now, innit?'

'Isn't it?' The correction came out automatically. We was back to that again. He saw the look on my face. 'Sorry,' he said. 'Sit down, Steve, my boy, and tell me what happened.'

I gave him a quick breakdown on events. At the end, he was cheering enthusiastically. 'You're a hero, my boy. A bloody hero.'

'Na,' I said. I was embarrassed with all that guff. I'm not used to it. 'What I need right now is a shower. I didn't half work up a lather racing through them streets.'

'Off you go then, Steve, my boy.' Dickie whacked me on the shoulder. 'And I'll see you later.'

I was half out of the door when I remembered. 'Oh,' I said, fumbling in my pocket. 'I picked these up off his desk when I was holding little old Krishna. Don't know what's in them.'

Dickie took the packets, and opened them up. He gasped and reached for his loupe. His face had regained its usual purplish hue, but went white again. 'God, Steve,' he whispered, 'Look at this sapphire. It's a Kashmir blue!'

I looked at the stone closely. As I say, I know nothing about gems, but am learning every minute. It looked good to me. It was a lovely deep blue colour, like cornflowers it was. Quite big too. I looked at Dickie. 'I think it's beautiful,' I said, hoping it was the right thing.

'Beautiful?' repeated Dickie. 'It's the most glorious gem I've ever seen. It must have come from Sri Lanka. It looks perfect to me. It's worth a small fortune.'

'Oh, good,' I said, not knowing what to say.

'Where did you get it exactly, Steve?' Dickie asked.

'I told ya. It, the packets, was on his desk as I picked him up. '

'Well, it's a very valuable stone. I suppose you should return it really,' he said.

I looked at him and he looked at me.

'On the other hand, Steve, my boy,' he nodded gravely, 'we were conned, weren't we?'

I nodded back. 'So – what shall we do?' Dickie went on. 'Shall we just take this as a parting gift from India?'

'Don't see why not,' I said. 'Finders keepers is what I say.'

'Quite, Steve. Quite.' He was already opening the second packet. Again he whistled. 'Steve, my boy, you've hit the jackpot again. Another emerald this time, not quite as good as the one I bought. But good enough. Good enough.'

He showed me the stone, which looked brilliant to me. 'Well, Steve, we'll have to give this extra windfall our serious consideration. You go for your shower, and we'll have a chat tonight over dinner in Delhi. We'll have a tip-top meal and celebrate. All right?'

Sounded good to me. I was half out of the door, when he called me back. 'Steve,' he was looking at me puzzled like, 'What made you show me these packets?'

'Whad'ya mean?'

'Well, you didn't need to. I would never have known you had them, would I? Why did you hand them over to me?'

'Dunno,' I said, and I didn't. 'Suppose it's like I'm working for you and that. They're yours really.'

Thinking about it, I was a bit surprised myself. 'Anyhow, you know all about these things, and I don't.' I turned to go. 'So it's only fair now, innit?'

This time he didn't correct me.

CHAPTER FIVE

MAGGIE

Back he came, as pleased as Punch, just as I was leaving for work. He was in high spirits, tanned, and looking fit. He said he felt a bit jet-lagged, and was going straight to bed. He promised to take me out for a slap-up dinner that evening – we always seemed to be going out for slap-up dinners when he was at home. Anyway, I had to go. I kissed him on the cheek and left. He seemed pleased to see me again – genuinely pleased. He kissed me back, not passionately – well, you could hardly expect passion at 9 o'clock in the morning, can you, after a flight back from India?

All day I thought about what I was going to tell him. I felt in the wrong as usual: I'd seen Alan a couple more times, and Steve had only been gone eight days. How things could change in eight days. Was I still in love with Steve? I didn't know any more. Alan was kind and gentle, and attentive: something Steve seemed to have lost the knack of being. I was in a right mess – I'd got two men, and yet I hadn't got anyone.

I met Janet for a sandwich at lunchtime, and told her the news. She had no doubts at all.

'I'd ditch him, hen, I would that,' she said forcibly. 'You're wasting your time with that one. Specially now you've got Alan in tow.'

'I haven't got him in tow. He doesn't come in to it,' I protested lamely.

'Whatever. Anyway, you'd better get yoursel' sorted, hen, or you'll end up with nothing at all.'

Janet always was a bit mercenary, but practical. I didn't want to lose Steve, yet I wasn't sure how I felt about him any more.

By the time I got back that evening, I'd decided not to say anything and see how things went. After all, if I told Steve, he'd hit the roof, and probably throw me out. He'd play the self-righteous one all right. I wondered about him, though. Had he been so pure himself while he was away? He was in the shower, whistling cheerfully. In a good mood then, that was good. I had a shower after him, dressed and then we went out to the Italian trattoria down the road. He was almost too cheerful. We ordered, and then I asked him how the trip had gone.

'Good,' he said cheerfully. 'Good.'

'Is that all?'

'Whad'ya mean?'

'Is that all you're going to tell me?'

'Nothing much to tell.'

I looked at him, my temper rising. 'Steve, you've just been on a trip of a lifetime. You've been to India. You've seen the Taj Mahal. You've seen all sorts of things. Yet, all you can say is 'good'.'

'Yes, well. I'm not so good at describing things, am I?' he said lamely. 'It's difficult.' He started to play with his knife.

'Right. Then let's take it bit by bit. What's it like – the Taj Mahal?'

'Oh, it's great. I mean it's brilliant. And so was the Amber Fort and that.'

'Amber Fort?'

Slowly I managed to prise it out of him, the main things he'd seen. Slowly he began to loosen up and unwind. I realised he must be tired after the flight, so his reticence was understandable. He told me about the poverty and how bright and colourful everything was; how it had rained a lot, but that it hadn't marred his enjoyment. He even spoke of the different religions, and how they were all mixed up together.

The meal passed pleasantly enough once he got started. He became quite voluble. I asked whether there had been any incidents.

'Whad'ya mean incidents?' he demanded suspiciously.

'Well, did anything happen to justify you being there in the first place?'

This made him mad for some reason. 'I dunno what ya mean,' he repeated. 'We was ever so pleased with the trip.'

'Good,' I said, and shut up. If he was hiding something, I wouldn't be hearing about it that night. Anyway, I was hiding something too, wasn't I?

'So,' he said, after he'd ordered dessert, 'What have you been up to?'

'Oh, nothing much. Working overtime, mostly. The washing machine broke down, and I had to get it fixed.'

'Oh yeh? Bet it cost a packet.'

'Not too bad. It was someone Janet knew.'

'That don't mean nothing,' he said, grumpily. He and Janet don't see eye to eye.

'They're splitting up,' I told him. 'Andy and Janet.'

'Not surprised. Andy's done the right thing.'

'It was Andy's fault actually. He's been unfaithful. He was seeing another woman.'

'Oh yeh?' Steve, looked at me strangely. 'How'd she find out?'

The conversation was taking the wrong turning, so I gave him the briefest explanation, which seemed to satisfy him. The meal finished peacefully enough.

He paid the bill, and we left. When we got to bed that night, he cuddled me for a while, just like old times. While I enjoyed his arms around me, I was feeling guilty as hell. Then he kissed me lightly on the mouth. 'D'you mind, sweetheart?' he said in apology, 'I'm feeling real tired with all the travel and that.'

'Course not.' I kissed him back. He turned over and went to sleep like a little baby.

I must say I felt quite relieved.

RICHARD

Every day I don't see Steve is a day wasted. It's two weeks now since we got back from India, and we haven't met, or even talked since. I've switched to answerphone; he's rung a couple of times and left a message, but I didn't reply. I have done this deliberately; I have to try and get him out of my system. Most people would say it's obscene for a 76-year-old man to be in love with a young man like Steve. But I am, and I must make sure I don't make more of a fool of myself than I have already. Our time together in India made me realise what a perfect pair we'd make if there weren't the age difference, and if my sex were compatible. So I sent him home to his Maggie: I've tried to do the right thing. It would be unfair to insist he stayed here with me. He wouldn't like it, and there's nothing for him to do here.

Our journey back on the plane was the pleasantest time I've had in years. We talked together for hours, giggling and laughing like two young kids. I still couldn't get over how brave he'd been in Jaipur and how he'd faced those men; but most of all, how he'd handed over the gems he took from Krishna's desk, without a second thought. It was Steve who suggested that, as I had so much extra luggage with the goods I'd bought in India, I should go through the Red Zone and declare whatever was necessary. He would saunter through the Green Zone with the gems. After all, we could afford to declare a few bits of silk and ivory when we had Steve's magnificent windfall to make up for it. So that's what we did.

Before we landed, Steve went to the loo and came out shaved, clean and fresh. He may be a lot of things but he's never scruffy. He had changed his T-shirt and looked very respectable and honest. It was about five-thirty in the morning, and I was not at my best: rather bleary-eyed and dopey. As it happened, this was to our advantage, as Customs homed in on me as if I were some common criminal. I showed them everything I had bought, and waited ages while the paperwork was done, and the bill presented. Finally I was allowed to go. I must say it had crossed my mind that Steve could meanwhile have done a runner with all the gems, so I was anxiously searching for him the minute I was through the exit.

But there he was, with his familiar, broad grin. We were met by the hire car I had ordered, and settled in the back for the long journey round the M25 and M20. Steve rummaged in the plastic bag holding his duty-frees and produced the packets of gems. 'There you are, matey,' he chuckled, well pleased with himself.

I couldn't believe he'd put them so casually at the bottom of the plastic bag: he's got nerves of steel, that one. He was smiling all over his face: 'Well, Dickie me lad,' he said, 'India'll never be the same again without us, will it?'

'You're a perfect partner in crime, Steve my boy,' I replied.

He looked quite hurt at this: 'Whad'ya mean crime?' he said. 'We wasn't doing no one no harm. Except for that git, Krishna. And he deserved everything that was coming to him.'

He was right in a way, but we had after all purloined two very valuable stones, which would more than pay for the trip; to say nothing of evading Customs and the dreaded VAT.

'Steve,' I began, trying to phrase the next question carefully.

'Yeah?'

'Promise you won't get angry with what I'm going to ask.'

'Oi, oi,' he said cheerfully. 'Now we're in for some home truths. Go on then, spill it out.'

'You won't get annoyed?'

'Nah.'

'Promise?'

'Go on then. I promise.'

'Well,' I started, 'Why do you always say "we was" instead of "we were"?'

There was silence for a while. 'Dunno,' he said finally. 'It's easier, I suppose. What's it matter anyway?'

'It matters, Steve, it matters.' I tried to explain. 'I know you think I'm just a stupid old snob, but the way you talk marks you, whether you like it or not.' He opened his mouth to say something, but I pressed on. 'Steve, you realise you've got a lot going for you, don't you?'

'Whad'ya mean?' His face had turned sullen.

'You're a good-looking, attractive man. You dress well. You have an attractive personality. You've got it all. But what will always hold you back, what will always mark you as – uneducated – is the way you speak.'

'I can't help -' he began.

'Oh, yes you can, Steve,' I assured him. 'I'm not talking about your accent – accents don't matter any more. You just make one or two glaring grammatical errors. If only you'd correct them, you'd sound a different man.'

Another long silence. Then: 'What grammatical errors then?'

I made out a list, and after I'd done so, I was surprised to see how short it was. Double negatives (which he found difficult), 'ain't', the additive use of 'and that', and the dialectical filler 'like', which drives me mad. This, however, I found impossible to explain. He just couldn't see what was wrong with beginning or ending a sentence with 'like' (let alone putting it in the middle for no reason at all).

He studied my list in bewilderment: 'Why Dickie?' he asked. 'Why is it so important?'

'I've told you, Steve, for your own good.'

Another pause. 'OK, Dickie me boy, if that's what makes you happy.' He grinned at me.

I tried to turn it around. 'It's to make you happy, Steve. In the long run.'

Having said all that, I wondered if I was right. Perhaps it really didn't matter one way or another. The more I tried to explain, the more confused he became; the more confused he became, the more out of touch with the modern world I felt. My heart went out to him struggling to comprehend something that made no sense to him, just to please me.

I dropped him off at his flat, and went home feeling lonely and sad; sad at being parted from the one person I really care about.

STEVE

What the hell is Dickie up to, like? I haven't heard from him for a couple of weeks now. I rung him a couple of times, but all I got was his plummy voice on tape. I left a message, but he didn't ring back. Why hasn't he rung me to take him to London with the gems? That's what I'm here for, isn't it, to be his minder and that. Now I'm seriously worried, and if I don't hear by tomorrow, I think I'd better go down and see if all's well. He could be lying dead in bed for all I know.

Life, if you can call it that, has got back to normal here in dreary old Ashford. I used to quite like living here, but now after my trips abroad, everything feels a bit flat. Relations with Maggie are a bit strained and all. I don't know what's the matter with her but she's not her bright, cheerful self no more. (Is that a double negative or whatever Dickie calls them? I still can't understand why it annoys him when I speak wrong. But he's well educated and I'm not, so he's probably right. He made it sound as if it was important for me, so at least I can give it a try. I dunno if I'll ever speak right though.)

Maggie doesn't seem to want to go out any more. She sits at home watching the telly, or doing the ironing, and says bugger all to me. It's as if we was – were- in different worlds. I don't give this relationship much more time. I keep thinking of Rana. Now there was a beauty for you, but she wasn't forthcoming neither. What's the matter with these women?

And then there's Janet. She's always in and out of the place, bawling away in that Scotch accent of hers. Now that she's left Andy – or rather Andy left her, wise man – she's got nothing better to do that give Maggie 'the benefit of her experience', as she puts it. A lot of old cobblers if you ask me.

So I'm hanging about doing nothing as if I was unemployed, which I'm not, ''cos Dickie's still paying in a cheque every week. Actually, that worries me a bit, ''cos if I was permanent like, I'd be paid monthly, wouldn't' I? Weekly makes you feel insecure, and I don't like it. I'm definitely going down tomorrow.

MAGGIE

Steve's like a cat on hot bricks. He's never still for a moment. He's restless and irritable, and I don't know what to do with him. Our relationship has deteriorated a lot, and I put it down to these trips abroad. How I wish he'd never met the old man. It seems I'm not to be introduced to him either. When they returned from India, the old man dropped Steve off at our door, but Steve never asked him in for coffee or anything. The car just sailed away, with Steve waving on the pavement. I happened to be standing at the window and saw this. I haven't said anything to Steve; whatever I say is seen to be a criticism, and he just snaps at me.

Janet's been round a lot, and has proved a mountain of strength. Her marriage is over, poor wee soul, so she's all by herself the now. When she comes here though, I'm between two stools with the pair of them. Steve and her just don't get on, but Steve doesn't understand what a good friend she is to me. Anyway, I don't come home to lunch any more: I say I'm too busy. I met Alan in the street the other day, and he asked when Steve was leaving again. He's taking it for granted we'll start up again as soon as Steve's back is turned. The awful thing is, we probably shall.

RICHARD

I couldn't stand it any longer, so I rang him last night and asked him down for lunch. I've got to see him, and talk to him and that, as Steve would add. I met him at Dover station and took him to a little restaurant in the town. It was very quiet there, hardly another soul in the place. He sat opposite me, smiling. He was well dressed in his casual way, always clean and smart.

'So, Dickie, me lad,' he began, 'what have you been up to?'

'Nothing much,' I replied. I could hardly say I'd been moping around the house all this time, accomplishing nothing.

'So how much did you get?' he demanded.

I was startled. 'For what?'

'Them gems.'

'Oh, those gems. Yes, of course.'

'Sorry,' he grinned. 'Those gems.'

I smiled back. He was trying. 'I haven't taken them up yet.'

His jaw dropped. 'You what?'

'I haven't had time,' I muttered, lamely. I could feel myself blushing. 'I've been busy.'

'I thought you said you haven't been doing much,' he looked at me accusingly.

'Yes, well,' I spluttered. 'There were other things to do.'

'So when are you going to take them?'

'Soon,' I said. 'Soon.'

He looked at me as if I were mad. 'You'll ring me, I suppose, when you decide,' he said.

'Well, I don't know – '

'Whad'ya mean you don't know? That's what I'm here for, innit? I can't have you wandering around London with all them gems in your pocket. You'd be mugged straight off.'

A great warm feeling came over me. He wanted to protect me. I know that's what I was paying him for, but he offered off his own bat. He wanted to do it.

'All right then,' I blinked. 'Let's say tomorrow then.'

'Tomorrow'll be fine. I'll come down in the morning.'

'No, no,' I said. 'You can catch the train at Ashford. I'll ring you to say which one I'll be on.'

He looked at me pityingly. 'That's all very well, Dickie, me lad. And what if you get mugged between here and Ashford? I'd never hear the end of it, would I?'

'It does seem a little silly,' I remonstrated, 'but if you insist -'

'That's settled then,' he said. He was in control, and he knew it.

We were having coffee after lunch, when he broached the subject I was dreading. 'So, Dickie,' he said, lighting a cigarette. 'When are we going to Samoa?'

'Samoa?' I pretended not to understand.

'Yeh. When you interviewed me, you said we was – were – going to Samoa.'

'Oh. Oh yes. Well. Do you want to go to Samoa?'

He stared at me. 'Does it matter what I want, Dickie? You're the boss.'

'Yes, well. I 'm not so sure now that we need -'

'So where are we going?'

'I'm not sure we're going anywhere.'

He was thunderstruck. 'You mean to say the job's finished? We've done it all?'

'Well,' I said, uncomfortably close to tears, 'there's not much point in Samoa now.' This was hardly true – the whole point of the exercise was for me to go to Samoa and do what I had to do.

'Why? I thought this was to be a permanent job?' he persisted.

'It was, Steve. It is.' I stammered. 'I took you on as my minder, and you certainly have been quite wonderful -'

'Well then?'

'It's just that – now we've become more than boss and hired hand, haven't we? We're friends.'

A long, disconcerting pause. 'So?'

'So,' I fumbled for the right words, 'I feel I can't continue with the employer/employee relationship. I – like you too much.'

Another long pause as he digested this. Then: 'Well I like you too, Dickie.'

My heart leapt. 'Yes, well – in fact, you're almost like a son to me,' I finished in a rush.

'So, what's the problem then?' he asked cheerfully. 'I pretended to be your son in Morocco, remember? And when I can speak proper, you'll be real proud of me. You're a cantankerous old sod at times, and I expect I get under your wick too. But I must say, Dickie, what we've been up to on these jaunts don't half give me a buzz. I want to carry on, if you do. And I promise to obey orders. You're still the boss, and I respect you for it.'

I gulped down my brandy and called for the bill.

STEVE

Blimey, there's a turn up for the books. I always knew Dickie fancied me, but I also knew he was a real gentlemen, and would never do nothing silly. At first sight I thought he was a dirty old man, but now I realise your feelings don't have to change just 'cos you get older. They just get pathetic – at least to young people, they do. In fact it's sad really – still wanting sex at that age, 'specially if it's another man you're wanting. 'Cos you're not going to get it, are ya? Chances are you might find some old bird wanting a shag, but not a guy. But what do I know?

On the way back home on the train, I thought about this a lot. I've never fancied a man – girls is much more my line, thank you very much. I remember me old mate, Jock, in London told me once when he was pissed that he was bi, and I'd laugh and wiggle me bum at him and that, but I've never felt that way. Well, perhaps once, many years ago, when I'd just left school in Penrith. We was in the shower, me and an old chum from school, who I knew was queer. We'd had a swim and we was drying off together. It was the sudden way he moved his shoulders sort of graceful like, with the towel draped round his waist. I felt the beginnings of an urge, which took me by surprise. I laughed for no reason, and flicked my towel at him; he gave a yelp, and that was the end of it.

But now Dickie's hinting that it's more than sex. He's saying he's in love with me and that. Well he didn't exactly say it, but it was obvious, wasn't it? And this bit about me being like a son to him. Course, if I play me cards right, I could be on to a good thing. On the other hand, he's a good-hearted old geezer, and I'm quite fond of him really. Nah, I couldn't do the dirty on Dickie. After all, he's given me a great time this last month or so, the old villain. That look of hope on his face when I said I liked him was quite touching really.

I got back to the flat in quite a cheery mood. Things were working out quite well, I thought, on the whole. Dickie had decided to go to Samoa after all, so me future was still secure. I had no worries he'd start to get heavy – whatever else he was, old Dickie was a gentleman. And there ain't many of those around these days, I can tell ya. The more I knew of Dickie, the more I liked and respected him. A right loveable old rogue he was and all.

And there was Maggie, sitting staring into space as if she was starring in some telly film like. My heart sank; I'm not one for getting depressed, but recently life in Ashford was getting me down. I couldn't do nothing right. Anything right. Oh, what the hell. Maggie's angry about something, and I'll hear about it before the night's out, that's for sure.

'What's up?' I enquired. Nicely, I thought.

She turned and glared at me, then turned back.

'What have I done wrong this time?' I tried again.

'Steve, we've got to talk.'

Oh God, how many times do you hear that on telly; it usually means they're about to break up.

'What about?' I said sitting opposite her.

'Are you happy with me?' She fired the first shot.

'Yeah. Yeah, course I am. Aren't you?'

'Steve, I've got to be honest with you -'

Another line from telly. Don't we say nothing original these days?

' – since you got this job with the old man -'

'Dickie,' I said. 'His name's Dickie. You never call him by his name. His name's Dickie.'

She stared at me. 'I didn't realise that was so important to you. Anyway, Dickie. Mr Grayson I should say, since I've never met him.'

'Didn't know you wanted to.'

'Didn't ask me, did you?'

This was getting nowhere 'What's the problem, Maggie?' I asked. 'Don't tell me you're jealous.'

'Have I reason to be?'

I had this weird feeling I wasn't watching telly, I was actually in it. In some soap that had a bad ending. Nobody was talking sense, just clichés. I knew I was doing this too, and didn't want to. I'm getting a right snob, and all.

I sighed and got on with the battle in hand: 'No reason at all. Can't think what ya mean.'

'I just wonder what you get up to when you're away. You never tell me anything. You could be doing anything.'

She was right there. 'Are you insinuating that I'm being unfaithful to yah? ' I asked in my high and mighty tone.

She was taken aback at this, and stuttered, 'No. Well no, not exactly.'

'Then what then?'

She began to cry. If there's one thing that gets on me nerves, it's when a bird starts to blubber.

MAGGIE

How can I explain what I mean? It's just that he's so secretive: I don't think he means to be, but he's holding back all the time. He asked if I was jealous, and I think I am. But of what? I was wanting to have a real cracking row with him to clear the air, but I can't, because I'm the guilty one, amn't I? I'm the one who's been unfaithful. Our relationship is on the rocks, and has been ever since he caught up with that old man.

I couldn't help crying: frustration really, unable to say what I was thinking and everything. Then he's away to the shower, and I could hear him singing chirpily. Next thing I know, he's telling me he's away up to London in the morning. Taking the old man on business.

'What business?' I asked.

'We – he's got some gems to sell, and I'm protecting him.'

'Gems? What gems?'

He sighed. 'Maggie, why do you always repeat what I say as a question?'

Never a straight answer. Always sidestepping the issue, dodging the subject. 'Why do you always avoid the question?' I countered.

'What question?'

I gave up. He always freaks out when I broach the subject of this bloody Dickie Grayson.

I started to make dinner, though I hadn't anything planned. Just cutting up veg and greens. Dinner would be a mess too, and it would be all my fault. Anyway, I concocted something, and we sat down to eat. He uncorked a bottle of wine. That was another thing: he never used to bother with wine, just stuck to his lager if anything.

The meal wasn't a success. I was sulking, or that's what he thought, and he didn't seem to want to say much. We finished the wine, which wasn't a good idea, as our tongues got loosened and then we said too much.

'We're going to Samoa next,' he announced.

I banged down my glass. 'Samoa?'

'There you again, Maggie. Repeating everything I say.'

'Well,' I said. 'That's quite a long way, isn't it?'

'South Seas,' he said, pleased with himself. 'South Pacific and that.'

'Oh,' I said. 'That'll be nice.'

'Yeah, won't it?' He got up and started to clear the table.

'Steve, I said. 'This isn't right.'

'What isn't?'

'You talking to me like this. So casual. As if I'd got nothing to do with it.'

He opened his mouth to reply, then thought better of it.

'Well then.' I stammered feebly.

'So you don't want me to go. Same as you didn't want me to go to Morocco. Same as you didn't want me to go to India. You just don't want me to go nowhere.' He steamed off to the kitchen.

I followed him in. 'It's not that, Steve,' trying to calm him down. 'It's just I'm not sharing with you. We're never together.'

He put the dishes in the sink and turned to me. 'Look Maggie,' he said putting his arms round me, 'I'm earning good money. Best I've ever done. You see that, don't you?

'Yes, of course, I -'

'Well then,' he said, as if that was all there was to it. 'I'm doing a good job, and being paid for it. Don't that make you happy?'

'Yes, of course, but -'

'Well then.' He turned back to do the dishes. End of conversation.

After we'd done the dishes, we went back into the living room to watch telly. I lit a cigarette. He looked at me. 'What's up with you, Maggie?' he said in surprise. 'You don't hardly ever smoke.'

I didn't answer, but sat staring at the telly. I was thinking of Alan, and all sorts of ideas came into my head. And Steve wasn't a part of them.

STEVE

True to my word, I got the train down to Dover the next day. Dickie collected me at the station, and we climbed up to the old white cliffs of Dover and along to his house in St Margaret's Bay. It was like them houses you see in old black and white war films, when they watch the Battle of Britain from their back gardens. It was a big house, with a huge garden right on the cliffs, with a view of the Channel that Maggie would die for. He must have a permanent gardener to cope with all them bushes and flowers and lawns and that. Dickie showed me around proudly, and gave me a coffee in the garden. We was sat on them comfy loungers they have round swimming pools abroad. This was the life all right – except it wasn't with my ideal kind of bird.

Dickie thought it was a complete waste of time and money for me to have come all this way down from Ashford to collect him, as we had to go all the way back again. Anyway, he collected the gem papers and drove us back to the Dover station. On the way up, he told me that plans for our South Pacific trip were going well: we'd be leaving in a couple of weeks, and be away for over month. Maggie will be pleased.

We got up to London without any problem at about one thirty. His appointment was at 2.15, but we was both hungry and looking for a bite to eat. Of course, the whole of London has to eat at the same time. We squeezed into one of them glorified sandwich bars, chock-full of Yuppies all talking about themselves. We gobbled down a couple of sandwiches and a cuppa tea which could have been made the day before, then got a taxi to an address in Greville street off Hatton Garden. Not an imposing street at all, in fact a bit tacky. It was a fairly modern building stuck between some grotty Victorian houses converted into jewellers' shops and that. We had to ring the bell and make ourselves known to security. We was ushered into a posh kind of showroom. Not the same as India at all. This man Dickie knew came in to greet us. He shook hands with Dickie, who then indicated me. 'And this is my colleague, Steven Jackman,' he said. 'Steve, this is Mr Nicholas Hoddesdon.'

I was right chuffed at that. Now I was a colleague. Right then, Dickie me lad, I said to myself, I won't let you down. I made up my mind to make an effort to speak proper and that. As it turned out, I didn't have to speak at all except to say 'pleased to meet you'.

It was an interesting meeting in more ways than one. The haggling this time was done at a more genteel level, with both of them smiling a lot and remaining gentlemen. At the same time, I began to notice that this Hoddesdon guy wasn't half twinkling at me. 'God,' I thought to meself, 'There goes another poofter. I seem to be flavour of the month.' Anyway, I didn't twinkle back, but gave a rather gracious smile, which stimulated him no end. I couldn't help noticing his white hands with long delicate fingers for a man. He handled the gems with such warmth and tenderness you'd think he was holding a dolly-bird's hand (well, not in his case perhaps). Anyway, the deal was soon closed after that, and the Hoddesdon guy offered tea.

'Thank you no, Mr Hoddesdon. Too kind, but we must be on our way.' Dickie had caught the twinkle and wasn't having any of that. A cheque was made out, hands were shaken and we left with smiles and twinkles all round.

Dickie took a taxi to the nearest branch of his bank to deposit the cheque, and then back to Charing Cross. Dickie was feeling the strain I could tell, but stations don't have seats any more, so we had to drink our cuppas standing up. He was complaining of a headache, and was relieved when it was time to catch the train.

We was alone in a first class compartment, when Dickie asked me if I'd enjoyed meself. I told him I had; it was definitely interesting but a bit above my head.

'But did you learn anything?' he went on.

'Yeah. I've learnt a lot from you and that. I can't talk like you and that, but I guess I have learnt a thing or two.'

'And you enjoyed it,' he persisted.

'Yeh, I said, didn't I? It was brilliant.'

'Right,' he said, and reached into his pocket. He brought out the sapphire I'd nicked from Krishna's desk. 'Remember this?' he went on.

'Yeah, of course I do.'

'Tell me about it then.'

'Well,' I tried to remember, 'You said if that ain't a Kashmir Blue you'd eat your loupe, or words to that effect, and that it was probably from Sri Lanka, and worth a fortune.'

'Well done.' he said, looking pleased. 'I may have exaggerated about it being worth a fortune, but it's a valuable stone all right.'

'Then why didn't you sell it with the others?'

He handed it to me. 'Present for you,' he said.

My mouth dropped open. 'You what?'

'I said it's a present for you.'

'But why?'

'Because you deserve it. And do close your mouth. Your manly charm is diminished somewhat when you do that.'

I didn't know how to thank him, and said so.

'Well, don't thank me' he snapped. 'Anyway, it's a kind of test.'

'Whad'ya mean?'

'Well, it's yours to do what you like with. You can either keep it, give it to your – er – Maggie, or decide to sell it at a profit. If the latter, then some time later on, we'll go back there with the sapphire. Only this time you'll do all the talking. You'll conduct the meeting. You remember the address, I trust, and the name of the man?'

I got real excited. I didn't think much of the idea of giving it to Maggie, which must give an indication of my real feelings. My life seemed to be opening up in new directions all at once. I went to the toilet, so that Dickie wouldn't see me jotting down the name and address of the dealer before I forgot it.

MAGGIE

He got back in time for dinner in a rare mood. His eyes were bright and sparkling; and for a moment I thought he was on something. He gave me a smack on the lips, and made himself a mug of tea.

'Good day then?' I ventured.

'Brilliant,' he said. 'Just great.'

'Dare I ask what happened?'

For once he was forthcoming, and poured his story out excitedly. They, or rather, Grayson had been selling gems up in London, and Steve gave an account of how the dealing had gone. I must say he seemed to know quite a lot about it, and I wondered why he hadn't told me some of this before. At the finish, he took this paper out of his pocket and unwrapped it for me to see.

My stomach turned over. 'That's never a sapphire, is it Steve?'

'Certainly is my girl.' He fondled it lovingly. 'Ain't she a beaut?'

'What are you doing with it then?' Was he, or were they both stealing or something?

'Dickie gave it to me,' he said proudly.

'Why?'

His smile faded. ''Cos I deserved it, that's why.'

My alarm grew. 'Why?'

His enthusiasm drained away. 'Maggie' he said, 'Why d'ya always do this to me? Why d'ya have to spoil things?'

That was unreasonable, I thought, and said so. 'What did you have to do to be given a sapphire, for God's sake?'

'Just my job, Maggie,' he said coldly. 'That's all. Just my job.'

'Which is?'

'You know what it is. You know what I'm doing.'

'That's just it, Steve,' I cried. 'I don't know what you're doing at all.'

'God, Maggie, sometimes you get so Scots. You get so negative and pessimistic. You're getting like your sister.'

'I am not, so there. What's Scots about that anyway?'

'Your native caution,' he said. 'Always scared to take risks.'

'No, I amn't. What risks? What are you talking about?'

'Just accept what I'm doing for what it is. An unusual job that's very well paid. You should be pleased.'

That night we went to sleep without speaking, something we'd never done before. We were growing so far apart now I didn't think it possible to repair the damage, and I wasn't at all sure I wanted to. Next day when I came back from work, I found he had bought a dictionary and a book on precious stones. Steve, of all people. I suppose I should have been pleased he wanted to better himself, but I wished for the old Steve back, with his cheerful smile and disposition.

Whenever I try to get close to him, I seem to be the dreary one, the one throwing cold water on everything, the negative one. And I was about to do it again. 'Improving yourself, I see,' I began with a smile.

'What's wrong with that?'

'Nothing,' I said, off on the wrong foot again. 'Want a cuppa?'

'Yeah.' He didn't look up. There was no smile, nothing.

I made the tea, and brought it to him. 'Steve,' I said.

'Yeah?'

'Look at me please when I'm talking to you.'

'Yes ma'am.'

'This isn't working, is it?'

'What isn't?'

'You know bloody well what isn't. Our relationship, that's what. It's gone to pieces.'

He looked surprised, but said nothing. 'Do you want to continue with me or not?' My voice was trembling as I came to the crunch at last.

'Course I do,' he answered, very matter-of-factly.

'Well, Steve, darling,' I went on, 'I'm not at all sure I want to.'

That did shake him. 'You what?'

'It's just not working, Steve, is it? Come on now, admit it.'

He didn't want to answer. It was clear I was the one who would have to make the decision; maybe he didn't want to hurt me, or maybe he just hadn't got the guts to say so.

I gave him my ultimatum: 'Well, let's do it like this. You're going away for a month you say. When you come back, perhaps you'll have the courage to tell me what you're really thinking.'

'And perhaps you will too,' he retorted.

Another evening passed in more or less silence. I couldn't wait for him to leave now, and I think he was feeling the same. I made my mind up about one thing though: I was going to see Alan again.

STEVE

The last couple of weeks have been hell on earth, I can tell you. Maggie has decided to leave me: she didn't say so in so many words, but it's what's on her mind all right. I suppose we haven't exactly hit it off recently, but I can't for the life of me think why. Our sex life is down to zero: she's cut me off completely. Sometimes I wonder if she's been seeing another bloke behind me back when I'm not there. Nah. That's not Maggie's style, she wouldn't do a thing like that.

Dickie rang at last to say we was leaving next Friday. There was to be a slight change of plan: he'd heard from Eric, who was safe and sound and on his way to Tahiti. We was to meet him there, and spend a week or so cruising round the islands, before going on to Fiji and that. Samoa and Honolulu would come later. Sounded good to me, though I wasn't mad about Eric Little by Little. Still, a cruise on a yacht wasn't to be sniffed at. I didn't need no injections or visas and that, so I busied meself with some shopping for clothes and stuff. I also tried to read a bit about gems, but it got complicated about minerals and all the different names they have for them. But I did learn about cutting and facets and that. I still haven't decided what to do with the sapphire Dickie gave me, But I won't rush into it; I took it to the bank and got me a safety deposit box. So it's in there till we get back.

I wish Maggie was more interested in everything, but there you go. It looks like we'll split when I get back. It's funny lying in bed beside her, and not getting me leg over. Don't seem much point really. The days pass real slow, and it looks like our departure'll never come; but of course it does. Time doesn't stand still, does it? Eventually the day dawns. Dickie would call for me about two o'clock. The flight wasn't until early evening, but he wanted to be sure we make it to Heathrow on time. It's a long flight: eleven hours to LA then on to Tahiti for another eight hours, arriving their time in the early morning. We were to stay at the Tahiti Hotel to get over the flight, and meet Eric the following morning. This was exciting by any standards, but Maggie just detached herself from it all. I bought a book on the South Pacific, and tried to get meself better informed – I didn't want to make a fool of meself in front of Sir Eric and that.

I got meself packed, and was waiting for Dickie when Maggie came back for her lunch break.

'So you're off then?' she said.

'Yeah.'

'Well, enjoy yourself.'

'I'll do my best. Sorry you're not coming too.'

'Are you?'

I sighed. She could be such a wet blanket. 'Maggie, can't you just wish me well?'

'Of course I do.'

But she didn't sound too convincing. Dickie's car drew up outside, the horn hooting. I gave Maggie a big hug – she didn't offer her face to be kissed. I felt her warm body and remembered the good times we'd had. It looked like it was all over. Seemed a pity to me.

'Bye, Maggie,' and kissed her hair.

'Bye, Steve.' Her voice was low, and when I let her go, I could see tears in her eyes.

MAGGIE

So he's away. I looked out of the window, saw him get in the car. He didn't look up or wave; too busy greeting his boss I suppose. The car drove off, and I sat down and cried.

Janet came round in the evening with the usual bottle of wine, and the drinking started. She said she'd seen Alan, and he'd been asking after me. Why don't I ring him, and get on with my life? Again why not indeed. It's awful to fall out of love with someone, and it's not easy to get over it. Yet I couldn't just shut the door like that. Maybe when he comes back – I'm kidding myself, I know, but you live in hopes.

Deep inside me I knew it was over, but I can't just get up and start another affair. Some people can fall in love on the rebound, but I'm not like that. I'm the stupid, faithful type: the one-man woman looking for a one-woman guy, as the song says. We got fairly drunk that night. I was waiting for Steve to ring from Heathrow, but of course he didn't. Now he was heading west into the great rosy future he'd created for himself.

Next morning I woke up with the biggest hangover of my life. I rang in to say I couldn't go in to work, and made some coffee. The doorbell rang, and it was Alan. He just stood there, smiling inanely, so I had to ask him in. I might have known Janet had rung him first thing to tell him the news.

I apologised for looking such a wreck, but he made the usual noises about me looking fine. I poured him a coffee.

'So what's your next step?' he asked.

'Step?'

'Well, Steve's gone for good, hasn't he?'

'Not quite,' I replied. 'Technically we'll make the final decision when he gets back.'

'Technically? You're going to wait that long?'

'I said I would,' I replied. 'But it's really hopeless, I know.'

'Then why not come out with me?' He reached for my hand.

'You mean, now?'

He laughed. 'No, not now. I mean soon. Tonight perhaps.' He was looking at me tenderly, and my heart sank. I was going to make another daft mistake.

CHAPTER SIX

RICHARD

He was full of excitement in the car, chattering away like a kid out of school. Once on the plane he quietened down a little, and we prepared ourselves for the long flight to LA. Air New Zealand served us a creditable dinner, and I certainly had my share of the champagne. After a coffee and brandy, I settled down to try and sleep. Steve wanted to watch some film or other: I can never see the point of straining one's eyes on that postage stamp screen stuck on your armrest. Anyway he was happy enough.

I put in my earplugs and snuggled down under the blanket, but sleep wouldn't come. The constant droning of the engines irritated instead of relaxing me. I could sense the proximity of Steve as he lay watching his film. My thoughts indulged in fantasy: I imagined him holding me close, his strong arms almost crushing me. My mind went beyond that, and merged into memories of Philip. My dear Philip. Sleep was impossible. I took off my earplugs and mask, and sat up preparing to read.

Steve was looking at me anxiously. 'All right, mate?'

I nodded miserably: 'Can't sleep. Must have drunk too much.'

'You were dozing at any rate. You was muttering away.'

'Oh?' I said anxiously. 'What was I saying?'

'Dunno. Couldn't catch it clearly. Some name like, over and over.' He was whispering so as not to wake the other passengers, and smiling sympathetically. 'Part of your past catching up with you, was it?'

'You might say that.'

'Want to talk about it?'

Strangely enough, I did. I had never imagined confiding my deepest secrets to a man such as Steve, but now he was the closest friend I had.

So I told him. I told him about Philip Hansworth. The American pilot I met at a Victory party in the summer of 1945. By then I was stationed at Dover, and went up to Town whenever I could. The war had just ended and everyone was on a high. I told him about how I fell in love with Philip, and he with me. About our wild affair that lasted the best part of a month. He was being sent back to the States, but he managed to get four days' leave just before his departure. He caught a train at Charing Cross and I met him at Dover station, where we found a taxi to take us to St Margaret's Bay and the Granville Hotel for four idyllic days and nights. The hotel was half way down a zigzag road to the pebbly beach. It was late August and the weather was kind to us. The scent of honeysuckle and jasmine and roses hung in the air. Everything was in full bloom and the world was returning to normal. I told Steve about our walks along the cliffs, looking out over the Channel. The bombs and air raids were no more; there was peace at last, and the whole world was rejoicing. We'd sit for hours just talking and gazing into each other's eyes. I told him about the hilarious evening Philip and I had at Noel Coward's house on the beach, and how we staggered back to the hotel as drunk as lords, and how we were locked out. We were twin souls. It was the highlight of my life and nothing has ever surpassed that wonderful long weekend.

'And that was the end of it then? You never saw him again?

'Oh, yes. I saw him intermittently for many years after that. He was married you see.'

Steve opened his mouth, but decided not to say anything.

'He was, in fact, already married when I met him in London. She, of course, was in America. But he would never divorce her. Catholic you see. Just wouldn't entertain the idea.'

'So what happened?'

'When he went back to the States, I thought it was all over. He would write – long impassioned letters about love and duty, with duty always winning. He loved her, I know, but the passion was with me. What a mixture of moralistic integrity and passion he was. Then one day in 1950 I got a call. He had come back to England with his wife, and was working at the Embassy.'

'Cor,' said Steve. 'The eternal triangle, eh?'

'In a way. But she never knew, at least in so many words. He was always loyal to her. And to me. He wouldn't do anything to hurt her.'

But it did hurt me. I couldn't help it. He would try and see me every day, or at least phone me, but always went back at night to his wife.

'Hilary. Hilary was her name. I met her once. Only once.'

I shan't forget that meeting either: talk about a woman's intuition. We met at Covent Garden in the interval. Philip and I had arranged it to look like a casual encounter, introducing me as an old wartime comrade. She sniffed the air as if it were poison. She was civil enough to me, but she sensed something all right. The meeting was not a success, and Philip and I decided to make no further efforts in that direction.

By then I had become an MP, and my career was taking off. I became Junior Minister, and my times with Philip became shorter and ever more difficult. I had bought my house in St Margaret's Bay on a sentimental whim, but I could never persuade him to come down and repeat that wonderful weekend we'd had. Then came the Profumo affair in 1963. Sex scandals were everywhere, and the press were out looking for blood. One day the Chief Whip called me in to his office to tell me the party had wind of my 'affair' with Philip. If the press got to hear of it, there would be repercussions for the US as well as the government. I felt sick at heart: they were going to ask me to give him up. But it was worse than that. They invented this other trumped up charge of taking money under false pretences. I had to resign: a matter of ill health and a personal letter from the PM saying how much I had done for the party and his sincere regrets etc. At the same time, Philip was mysteriously recalled to the States, and left almost without being able to say goodbye.'

'Blimey, you are a dark horse and no mistake.' Steve's mouth was still open. I had to smile. 'So that was that then?'

'More or less,' I replied. 'I never saw him again. But I always loved him. I still do.'

'Where is he now then?'

'He's dead,' I replied. 'He died in 1966.'

'What about his wife?'

'She's still around. She lives in San Francisco in the old family house. Funnily enough, she sends me a Christmas card every year. Now he's dead I suppose she feels she has nothing to be worried about.'

'No kids?'

'No. I never knew why. Philip would never talk about his sexual relationship with Hilary. I don't know why they didn't have children. As I said, he was intensely loyal to both of us.'

Going back over my life and love for Philip effected a tender sadness, then drowsiness over me. This emotional catharsis had left me drained, and I slipped into a gentle sleep.

STEVE

Poor old Dickie. He looks so old and pathetic lying there with his blanket up to his chin. It's funny how your ideas change. In the old days, I was as ready as the next one to send up the poofters. Not to hurt them, mind. Let them do what they liked, as long as they didn't interfere with me. But I thought they was fair game. But now I could see that Dickie had loved as much as any man can love, and had suffered more than most. Poor old sod. At least he's had a great love – I'm not so sure I've had that yet meself.

There was old Cynthia, of course. That's a few years back now. I was too young for a long-term relationship then, but somehow got dragged into one just the same. It's always the way, isn't it? It's there when you don't need it, but never when you do. Cynthia was great really, but twelve years older than me. She had more of a problem with that than I did, 'cos she kept talking about her biological clock, although she wasn't that old. She got herself pregnant by me all right, and was thrilled to bits until she had a miscarriage. God, I don't want to go down that road again, thank you very much.

She was inconsolable, her friends said, and nothing I could do seemed to help her. It went on week after week, month after month, this deep grief. Everyone rallied round her; trying to help. She was sent for counselling, but that was no good either. And all that time no one thought of me. I was the father, you know. I had feelings too, you know. It was my kid that died and all. Nobody thought of counselling me. In the end she sent me packing, and I was glad to go: we were getting nowhere, and never would. I was only like 26, wasn't I? After that, I just went from one bint to another, trying to enjoy life the way you're supposed to. But there was never anything serious until I met Maggie. And I really cared – care for her like. Dear old Maggie is great, but as for true love? And now, after a year and all – for the rest of my life? I don't think so.

The aircraft lights were switched on and they were serving us a snack and that. We'd soon be landing in LA. The pilot announced we was flying over Las Vegas. I looked out of the window to see that incredible sight: it was like fairyland, with all the hotels blazing away with lights. The blues and greens of the swimming pools and that stood out against the darkness of the surrounding desert.

We landed safely, and were bustled through a corridor straight onto another plane bound for Tahiti. It wasn't long before we took off again, and blow me down, they served us another dinner. My body clock was going through a hard time I can tell you. Eventually we settled down to sleep. Dickie had scoffed down his usual ration of champagne, but hadn't eaten so much.

This time I couldn't sleep. For no apparent reason, I was getting a hard on. Well, there was a reason, actually. One of the stewardesses had been giving me the eye, and I was wondering if there was any chance of going to the rear of the plane and having it off with her in the toilet. I didn't know if that was on or not, but was debating the matter to meself, when Dickie interrupted my thoughts to ask me:

'How did you meet Maggie, Steve?'

If ever there's a way to dampen the hots over one girl, it's to start talking about another. I sighed and gave up the idea of the stewardess.

'I was doing odd jobs on the roads like I told you. I was living in London at the time, when my mate, Jock, had to deliver some goods down at Ashford. He asked me along for company as I wasn't doing noth...anything, and was out of work as usual. He did his deliveries, and we stopped in a caff for a bite to eat, when this bird, Maggie, came in with her hell-cat sister, Janet. They saw we was interested and were laughing and giggling away fit to bust.'

'So you picked her up?'

'Would have done, given half a chance, but she was playing hard to get.'

I remember that day so well. God, she was a piece of something all right. She wore her red hair long, and her pale skin was...translucent, like some of them gems we saw in India. There was a slight resemblance to her sister, I suppose, both having red hair and that, only Maggie was all soft and gentle like – the peaches and cream variety, while Janet was crab apple tart. We followed them out of the caff and along the street and then into Sainsbury's. So in we went as well. We could hear their Scots accents, so it was Jock who started the conversation seeing as how he was Scots as well.

He fancied Maggie all right, but Maggie was looking at me. Finally I spoke to her, and asked her name. She fixed me with those green eyes of hers, and smiled. She said her name was Maggie. I fell for her that instant.

'But you lived in London you said.' Old Dickie was looking puzzled.

'Yeah. Like I said, I fell for her real hard. I told Jock I'd make me own way back to London, and ring him later. He wasn't best pleased, I can tell ya.'

'I should think not,' said Dickie with pursed lips. 'He'd asked you there to keep him company.'

'Yeah, I know. But you gotta do what you gotta do.'

She gave Janet her marching orders, and we walked and talked all over the place. I was feeling really horny by then, and going out of my mind for it. She asked me back to her place for a cup of tea.

'Tea was the last thing on my mind, I can tell ya, Dickie me lad. But I sure went back to her place.'

It was the same little flat that we was to share together for this past year or so. More like a bedsit, or studio flat, but it had a biggish kitchen you could eat in and a bathroom. Just the one living room with a bed in it.

'Anyway, one thing led to another as you might imagine, and the bed was definitely the most used article of furniture, if you catch my drift.'

'Only too clearly.' said Dickie, a bit sarcastically I thought.

'Well, I didn't go home that night, or the night after. And eventually we decided I'd move in with her, seeing as how I had nothing doing in London. So that's what happened.'

'And what about Jock? Your mate? Wasn't he upset?'

'What about? He was all right. We're still great mates.'

Dickie digested this, trying not to look disapproving. 'I see,' he said at last. 'Jolly romantic.'

'Suppose so. What drew us together, I suppose, was the fact we had both lost a child.'

'You had a child?'

'Yeah, with Cynthia. I told ya. Many years before.'

He nodded. 'You told me about Cynthia – not about the child.'

'Yeah, well.'

'How terrible for you. For you both, I mean.'

'Yeah. It's the woman that gets all the sympathy, though. I was hurting too, you know.'

'Steve, I'm so sorry. You're still hurting now, aren't you?'

'Dunno. Sometimes, it just don't seem right – both of them having miscarriages and that.'

'It's hardly your fault though, is it?'

'Dunno. Sometimes I feel it is – though Maggie's child was nothing to do with me. Anyway, that's what kept us brought us together, Maggie and me. We could both understand the other's grief. But sometimes I think it was just sex.'

'So what happens now?' he asked. 'When we get back, I mean.'

'God knows,' I replied.

Dickie half-smiled at me and went to the toilet. I tried to doze. Roll on Tahiti and those dusky maidens.

RICHARD

The flight seemed to last forever, but Steve regaled me with his story of how he met Maggie, although I was somewhat shocked to hear of his earlier affair with Cynthia. I think the loss of his child has affected him more than he will admit to, and now it looks as if Maggie and he are going to break up, and I feel guilty for feeling pleased.

Finally the lights in the aircraft came up, and we were told we'd be landing in half an hour. God knows what the local time was. I hadn't changed my watch when we got to LA, so it was hours behind. I felt very bleary-eyed indeed, but Steve was looking his usual cheeky self. We landed at Tahiti at last, and the soft exotic air of the tropics hit us at once. The effect is immediate; one relaxes and gives oneself up to the languorous life style of French Polynesia.

Steve rounded up our luggage, and led the way to the taxi rank. I was too far gone to be of much use: I felt utterly drained after all those hours in the air. I had booked us into the Hotel Tahiti – not the best on the island, but it was between the airport and Papeete, where we were to join Eric that afternoon. By the time we got to the hotel it was nearly 3 a.m., and we were to meet on the Annabella for lunch that afternoon. I left Steve to his own devices and fell into bed and a deep refreshing sleep.

I woke about nine o'clock feeling a lot better, so I ordered some breakfast in my room, then showered, dressed and went to look for Steve. He was lying by the pool, looking irritated – unusual for him.

He grunted a greeting.

'What's the matter with you?' I asked.

'Jet lag, I suppose. Didn't sleep a wink. The traffic never stopped all night.'

'What traffic?'

He sighed. 'On the road traffic, of course. Your humble servant had a room facing the road.'

'Oh.' I didn't know what to say. 'Sorry about that.' Steve was now used to the best hotels, and had upgraded his essential requirements. It's true this hotel was past its prime, but it had once been the residence of a Tahitian princess, and still retained much of its charm. I thought it would be a good introduction for Steve to the South Pacific.

'Yeah, well. There it is.'

'Have you had breakfast?'

He had. There was a sudden shower, which displeased him even more. I decided to assert myself. 'Good,' I said, briskly. 'Then let's get going.'

'Where to?'

'To buy some pearls. Tahiti 's famous for its black pearls.'

'I thought we could just lie here until it was time to meet the boat,' he muttered.

'Yacht, not boat. And we can't. There's only just time to do some shopping, so get dressed, and let's be on our way.'

He got up with bad grace, and ambled into the hotel. But he came back quickly enough, and we took a taxi into Papeete. The sun had come out again, and the streets were bustling with activity. Steve brightened up a little, and even managed a grin at a couple of girls standing on the corner. I took him first to the Tahiti Perles Centre, which was almost opposite the yacht marina.

'There it is,' Steve pointed. And sure enough there was the Annabella, but no sign of anyone on board.

I took him into the museum of the history of pearls, and Steve came to life again. He listened attentively to the explanation on how these pearls are farmed. He really appears to be attracted to jewels, and looks at them with appreciation, not avarice. I explained that this was a highly reputable shop, and so the prices were too high. We strolled along the Boulevard in brilliant sunshine; it was almost too hot for me, but Steve was thriving on it. He was his old perky self again. Thank God.

We turned off the Boulevard into a smaller shop, where I'd done business before. Our time was limited, so we got down to it immediately. My knowledge of pearls is inadequate, but I explained to Steve (although he had learned most of this already at the museum) that these pearls came from the giant black-lipped oyster, and take at least three years to form. A good pearl should be round, smooth and flawless, reflecting a blue or green grey colour. I finally bought a beautiful grey green pearl, which looked flawless to me. I paid for it in US dollars, and gave it to Steve to take care of. We had a coffee and wandered about a bit before returning to the hotel to collect our luggage and meet Eric on the yacht. I wasn't looking forward to this part of the trip: we were nearing the end of our time together and I wanted Steve all to myself. But I couldn't refuse Eric's invitation.

And the time was drawing near for me to tell Steve the truth, and I was dreading that.

STEVE

Jet lag was giving me the willies. I felt I hadn't slept for days. What was left of the night we arrived in Tahiti I spent listening to traffic outside my window. My head was thick as a hangover when we left the hotel and drove to the marina to board Eric's yacht. Richard was being difficult and bossy. He knew bloody well I was feeling poorly, but he kept needling me all the way. An added annoyance was that everybody spoke French, and some only a little English.

'This is French Polynesia, you know,' Dickie rubbed my nose in it.

We finally boarded the boat, and there was Eric, skipper's cap on head, smiling his smarmy smile and showing his expensive teeth. All the same he looked his age – he was walking with a stick, and with difficulty. There was a lot of hugging if not kissing between the two villains before we were ushered below to the saloon and the blessed air-conditioning. The cool air perked me up at once and when my eyes got used to the gloom, I made out a figure lying on the sofa: Yolanda.

She was introduced to me as Yolanda Gibbons, Eric's granddaughter. She was Claudia's heiress, and therefore as rich as they come. But that wasn't all the good news. She was drop-dead gorgeous. The bad news was that as she was filthy rich, she was spoiled rotten by her grandfather and anyone who came near her. But what a body, to say nothing of the face.

She was in one of them sarongs, or pareus as I later found out they was called; it was flimsy enough to lead you on no end. It was white with huge dark blue flowers on it, which showed up her eyes – the colour of sapphires. She had long blond hair, which looked to be real, and smooth tanned skin .She wasn't tall, but everything was just right, including a splendid pair of boobs, straining through that wispy material.

I shook her hand. It was soft, yet firm, and was that a slight twitch of those long fingers an invitation? 'Hi,' I said.

She smiled back through her hot red lipstick. 'Hello.'

Unfortunately, we was eating on deck under an awning. I'd have preferred the air-conditioning meself, but my opinion wasn't called for. I didn't say much at lunch – too busy eyeing Yolanda and having a right good fantasy. She caught me looking at her several times, and I was thinking this was going to be some cruise. I noticed that Eric was careful about what he said in front of her, so obviously she knew nothing about his smuggling activities. Dickie never mentioned them, and didn't even ask what had happened at Gibraltar. We'd find out soon enough, I expect.

After lunch, when Dickie and Eric called for another bottle of wine, I 'd had enough: I said I wanted to shake off this jet lag bit, and be at my best that evening. Eric told us his plans: we were leaving Tahiti that afternoon and making for the island of Moorea, which you could see wasn't far away. Then we was going to Bora Bora and Huahine, and then we'd see.

I went below to my comfy cabin and tried to sleep: but the thought of Yolanda and an accompanying erection put a stop to that, and in the end I went up on deck again. I'm glad I did too.

RICHARD

Eric and I were left alone eventually. Yolanda (my, how she'd grown – I hadn't seen her for years, of course) and Steve had drifted off to their respective cabins, and at last I could hear what had happened to Eric. His laconic explanation on the phone had been far from clear, so I was agog for news.

'I've changed a lot, Richard,' he began.

I could see that: he looked ten years older. 'What happened, Eric?' I asked.

'It was the Gonzalez gang,' he replied.

I thought so; they had caused trouble before. A kind of Spanish Mafia, they were taking over the whole of the western Med. There had even been clashes with the Italian Mafia and Camorra.

'When you and Steve had gone, I went down below for a snooze. I told the crew to clear up, and then gave most of them permission to go ashore for a couple of hours, leaving Ferdinand, the Filipino, on watch.'

He lit a cigarette, trying to control his trembling hands. So he'd started to smoke again. 'Three of Gonzalez's boys came on board, and Ferdinand didn't stand a chance. Although I sometimes wonder if he was in on it. He scarpered after it was all over. I haven't seen him since.'

'So what did they do to you?' I asked gently.

'The usual working over. They tied me up, and told me politely that I'd been warned off their patch, but had chosen to take no notice. Then they gagged me so that no one would hear me scream, and broke my right foot. It will never heal properly. I'm too old you see.' His voice shook.

I couldn't bear it: the great successful Eric, now helpless and vulnerable. 'Oh Eric,' I said uselessly.

'I lay there after they left, until one of the crew came back early and found me. He called for an ambulance; I told him not to call the police, but they came anyway. I was in hospital for the best part of two weeks. When I was well enough to get back to the Annabella, I was told by the authorities I was persona non grata, and to leave at my earliest convenience. Always an amusing turn of phrase that.' He attempted a smile.

I leaned across the table and took his hand. 'I'm so sorry, Eric. I really am.' I muttered, aware of the first physical contact I had ever made with him.

'So now, as I said, I'm a changed man,' he was making a great effort. 'I've finished with all that. All the smuggling and dope running. I didn't really need to, you know. I'm well enough off. It gave me a thrill, though. And we had some good times, didn't we?' His old smile burst forth as he squeezed my hand.

'Oh Eric, we certainly did.'

'I'm sorry, though, I can't help you any more. I've given it up.'

'Don't worry on that score,' I said. 'I've more or less given it up too.'

He smiled his old smile. 'Thanks for coming, Richard. I really appreciate it.'

'We were coming to the Pacific anyway,' I said.

'I know. But I needed to see you. At times like these, old friends are best.'

'So what are you going to do now?' I asked to change the subject. I knew he hated sentimentality, and would regret later what he'd said.

'Well, for the moment, not much. You know, Yolanda and I have a lot in common, strange as it might seem. We understand each other, and have few secrets, apart from my nefarious deeds with drugs, although she must have some suspicions -she's not exactly stupid. Anyway, she's recovering from her divorce, and I from my beating. We'll comfort each other and potter around the South Seas for a while. I expect I'll pick up the odd pearl or two to take home. Just to keep my hand in.' His eyes had taken on their customary brightness again. The sad truth of it was he loved his 'game' – for that's what he considered it to be – of smuggling , and I suspect he'll be lost without it.

'You might know,' he laughed, 'that after they beat me up, they scarpered with all that cannabis and heroin that Steve had so heroically saved. You'd better not tell him that.'

'What's that then?'

I turned, and there was Steve coming up from below. I explained briefly, giving him a warning look not to ask too many questions in front of Eric. He understood, thank goodness, and smiled at Eric for the first time. Eric rose to go, and leaning on his stick, apologized for leaving us. 'It's my turn now to have a siesta,' he said. 'We'll be leaving in the early evening.' He turned to Steve. 'I'd like you and Yolanda to see the sunset over Moorea.' Another smile and he hobbled down the companionway.

I was feeling a bit dopey myself, as Eric and I had downed quite a lot of wine between us. We had always been good at that. I filled Steve in with what had happened to Eric, and he nodded in sympathy.

'Thought it was something like that,' he grunted. 'Bastards.'

'Yes, well, that's what comes of dealing with crooks,' I said. 'Let that be a lesson to you.'

'You what?' He cried, half smiling, half in earnest. 'Who's been gallivanting round the world, teaching me immoral tricks then?'

'Not immoral – amoral. Immoral usually concerns sex, and I certainly haven't taught you anything in that field.'

He digested this. 'Whatever,' he said. 'Anyhow, you can't say you're exactly honest now, can you?'

'I never hurt anyone,' I answered.

'Except Krishna in India,'

'Come on, Steve, you were there. You agreed with what we should do.'

He grinned. 'Yeah, I know. Just kidding.'

I left it at that. Something was bothering him. I'd find out sooner or later. We exchanged smiles, and I went down to my cabin.

STEVE

I could see Dickie was half pissed as he staggered downstairs to his cabin. He was grinning idiotically and indulging in little belches and a fart or two. He seemed happy enough, but he wasn't on top form. Neither was Eric. You wouldn't think Gibraltar was only a couple of months' ago from the way they was both acting. Eric I can understand – being beaten up like that, but Dickie – I reckon he drinks too much, to say nothing of eating. I wish he'd sober down a bit. Sometimes I think he's on self-destruct.

The sun was beating down the way it does in the tropics, although there's always clouds over the mountain peaks that dominate Tahiti. I looked over to Moorea, where we were going later. It looked mountainous and jagged over the Sea of the Moon, the stretch of water separating us. it couldn't be much more than ten miles away. I walked along the deck to the bows, and there was Yolanda, in her bikini but topless, giving me the benefit of her glorious boobs, which were bursting with health in the sun.

'Hi,' I said to start the conversation like.

'Hello,' she answered but not looking at me, concentrating on her tan, although I couldn't see how she could get much browner.

'Mind if I join you?' Why is it I can never think of anything original to say when I want to impress?

'Grab a mattress,' she waved an arm at the loungers spread in readiness.

I lay down as near to her as politeness would allow, and took off my shirt. I wished I'd changed into my swimming gear, but there would be other times I hoped. Mustn't rush things. The rustling of my shirt coming off alerted her to danger or whatever, and the sunglasses were removed. She sat up, twirling the shades between two fingers.

'Want some cream?' she said.

'Cream?' I repeated stupidly.

'For your sunburn. Or what will be sunburn if you don't put some cream on.'

'Oh. Yeah. Thanks.'

Her hand touched mine as I took the tube. Her perfume hit me below the belt. Just as well I wasn't in my trunks.

'Want me to rub your back?' She leant over.

I turned over onto my stomach with some relief, I can tell you. We hadn't left the harbour yet and already I had an erection like those mountains sticking up over the water. God knows what'll happen tonight.

'So,' she said, after she'd worked me up to a right lather, 'tell me about yourself.'

'Whad'ya want to know?'

'Well, first and most important, what are you doing with Richard?'

'Doing?'

'You know what I mean. Are you his catamite?'

'His wha -?'

'Or stud?'

'I dunno -'

'In short are you gay?'

'Course not.'

'Bi perhaps?'

'Not even.'

'How can you be so sure?'

''Cos I've thought about it.'

'Have you indeed? Why was that? You must have doubts if you thought about it.'

She was beginning to get under my wick. 'Whad'ya asking all these questions for anyway?'

'I just want to know where I stand.'

Now that sounded hopeful, so I gave her a grin. 'Where do you want to stand then?'

'That can be discussed later. But what are you doing with Richard if you're not "serving him", so to speak?'

I grinned even more. 'Well, I am serving him,' I said. 'But not in the way you think.'

'You mean you're his servant.'

That didn't sound right either, but I suppose it was true. 'Yeah, in a manner of speaking.'

'So what do you actually do for him?'

'Look after him and that.'

'What does "and that" mean?'

She was really riling me now. 'What I say. He's an old man, and needs looking after. What are you going on about it for?'

She looked at me, her red lips pursed but luscious. 'Just checking, that's all.' She lay back again on her mattress, closed her eyes, and put back her shades. Evidently the conversation was over.

We lay like that for quite some time, although I was feeling really uncomfortable, and trying to think of a way to leave without looking an absolute prat, when she started again.

'Married?'

'You wha -?'

'Are you married?'

'No. Are you?'

'Divorced, or in the middle of. Why aren't you married?'

'Whad'ya mean?'

'Why do you keep saying "Whad'ya mean" when it's perfectly obvious what I mean? You speak English don't you? You're a well set-up sexy-looking guy, well over thirty. So what's the catch?'

This was getting nasty. 'No catch. I'm a normal hetero, who ain' – isn't married, that's all. If it's got anything to do with you, I am deep in a relationship at the moment.'

As soon as I said that, I regretted it. My chances wouldn't be up to much if she thought was accounted for. 'Anyway, 'I hurried on, 'people don't get married so fast these days, or hadn't you noticed?'

She ignored my last bit. 'What's she like?' she demanded.

'She's beautiful. Red hair, pale complexion.'

The thought of Maggie felt good now I was so far away.

'How long have you been with her?'

'A while.'

'Going to marry her?'

'You're obsessed you are. You're obsessed with marriage.'

She lay down again. I couldn't tell if she was offended or not, and I was beginning not to care. The shades went on again. I turned back on my stomach, more for the sun than necessity this time. My erection was quite gone.

There were stirrings all over the yacht; the crew were busy with ropes and things, the engines were throbbing and Captain Eric came up from below. We were leaving Tahiti and on our way across the Sea of the Moon to Moorea. I put my shirt back on and leaned over the rail to watch proceedings.

MAGGIE

I was in two minds whether to go out with Alan that night or no. But of course I did. There seemed little else to do. He's a nice guy right enough, thoughtful and considerate, but I don't know. What's the point of getting involved again, when he'll leave me in six months, a year, whatever?

Janet had asked me to meet her that night, so that we could have another depressing evening feeling sorry for ourselves. She was looking forward to a wine-sodden night with true Scots gloom. I rang her at work to say I'd had second thoughts and that it wasn't such a good idea, but she'd left the hospital and was already on her way round.

In she came, all guns firing, cursing Andy and what he had done to her, cursing Steve for what he had done to me. She mashed some tea, and sat down to discuss future strategy

'Maggie,' she began, 'I've got the perfect solution. It's stupid you living here, and me leaving there. Why don't we combine forces and live together? It'll be like old times.'

Dear God, what a thought. I'm very fond of my sister, she's a good wee soul, and will do anything to help you, but to live with her would be hell on earth. 'I don't think -'

'It'd cut doon our expenses too, you ken. Two's cheaper than one tae feed.' she rattled on enthusiastically.

'Janet,' I broke in, 'it's kind of you to think of it dearie, but at this moment, I just want to be my myself a while.'

'Oh aye,' she said. 'I didnae mean the now, but when you're broken off completely with Steve.'

'Yes, well,' I said lamely. 'It's quite a big step to leave him, you know, and it'd be another big step to share with you, so – '

Just then the bell rang, and who should it be but Alan calling for me to take me out.

STEVE

It didn't take long to cross the Sea of the Moon, and when we turned into the north side of Moorea and lost sight of Tahiti, another world opened up. This was much more like my idea of the South Seas. We passed a fabulous lagoon with water a colour I've never seen before: talk about sapphire blue. But it was also emerald green and clear, so clear. I'd never seen a coral reef before: they're amazing. It's like having a pearl necklace round you, like a moat, protecting you. We were sailing towards Cook's Bay into the sunset. And that was something else. We'd all been laughing and joking and that, but when we saw that sunset, we all went quiet. The sea seemed to go on forever and joined the sky all yellow and gold with the clouds dark grey and lavender. I'd never thought of colour much before I met Dickie, and he introduced me to the gems and that, but what with them and these natural colours of sky and sea and all, I felt something else.

They cut the engine, and everything was silent. No one spoke, and we all just watched the sun sink ever so fast down the horizon. Just the sound of water lapping the side of the yacht. There were other boats out from the Bay to watch too. Then we sailed into Cook's Bay, which was another great bit of scenery. It was surrounded by these mountains with peaks jagged like bread knives, and one great mountain sticking up proud like a giant's molar. Mt. Rotui I found out it was called, and wherever you went in Moorea, there it was often surrounded in cloud it was so high. I found it beautiful.

We anchored in Cook's Bay; cocktails were served and conversation returned to the usual stupid meaningless remarks. I felt right out of it, with all of them chattering away like blue-arsed monkeys, flashing their sophistication. Eric was on about this painter guy, Gauguin in Tahiti and Post-Impressionism and synthesism. This led him on to a lecture on modern art and surrealism with Dali. I couldn't get the hang of it all, but made sure I'd look those words up when I got to my cabin, in case they started in on it again tomorrow. I just wanted to sit quiet like, and look at the view. I thought of the Taj Mahal in India, and now this. They made me feel different like. I felt I wanted to do something different: change meself in some way, but I didn't know how or what way I wanted to change.

We were ferried to the Club Bali Hotel for dinner, which was another noisy business. There was a crowd of Americans sitting at a huge round table, drinking and cracking jokes, as if they was in a McDonald's or something in Dallas. The evening was soft and gentle, the scent of pineapple and that was everywhere. What the hell had they come for?

It finished finally, and we were all ferried back again to the yacht. But now Yolanda was showing signs of the drink she had swallowed in large quantities, to say nothing of Dickie, who had had more than his quota. Eric was still quite sober, but I was the only one who seemed affected by the night and our surroundings. Nothing seemed to have touched the others at all. Dickie said goodnight to me blearily; his speech slurred and incoherent. He was unsteady on his pins, and asked me to help him to his cabin. I must have looked disapproving like,"cos he took me by the hand and murmured 'Sorry. Sorry, Steve.'

'That's all right, mate,' I said as cheerily as I could. 'That's what I'm here for.'

'It isn't really though, is it?' He was sitting on his bed looking terrible.

'Are you all right, Dickie?' I was a bit concerned about him.

'Yes, I think so. I'm drunk.'

'I can see that.' I grinned at him and turned to go.

'Steve,' he said sharply.

'Yeah?'

'I've got to talk to you.'

'What about?'

'Important. About important things. Matters of great concern.' He half giggled and yet looked serious. 'Tomorrow when I'm sober. All right?'

'Sure,' I said. 'Whatever you say. Night then.'

'Night, Steve.'

As I left, he was staggering to his feet to go to the toilet. I felt a bit guilty leaving him like that. But I couldn't very well do much else. Also what did he want to talk about? He sounded serious like, and a bit ominous. Was my job on the line again?

But our talk wasn't to be the next morning. Dickie was still feeling sick, and wanted to stay in bed for a while. There must be something wrong with his stomach: he's always being sick these days, and it can't always be food poisoning. By now we had anchored in Robinson's Cove in the next bay round the corner. Eric had booked a Jeep to take us round the island, and we set off about ten o'clock in the morning – just me and Yolanda, Eric and a local female guide built like a tank. Dusky maidens seem to be in short supply.

The car took us up a steep road to the belvedere to look at this incredible view of Opunohu Bay and Cook's Bay with Mt. Rotui towering between them. The sea stretched out in the distance, disappearing in a heat haze. Underneath us was a forest of trees with the mountains falling on either side to the sea. Nearby was a place sacred to the old warrior chieftains. It was quiet and peaceful among the chestnut trees as the guide went on a bit about their past history. She showed us a lipstick tree (that's what she called it), and showed us how the (presumably) dusky maidens reddened their lips with its flower. Yolanda immediately had a go, and smothered her already red mouth with the stuff. We all wandered about for a bit. A tour minibus had followed us up and was now disgorging its passengers onto the belvedere. I went off on my own to have a look at one of the ruined temples down the track.

And there was Yolanda, standing quite still under an old tree, gazing into space. I was hesitating whether to speak or not, when she turned and saw me. 'Hello' she said, and gestured me to sit by her.

We sat there in silence for a while. I was surprised, 'Cos I didn't think she was the sitting quiet sort of girl. She let out a deep breath and looked at me. 'It makes you wonder what we're all doing here, doesn't it?' she said.

I was thinking the same, but didn't know how to say so, so just nodded silently. 'Have you ever been in love, Steve?' she asked.

'Yeah, I suppose so,' I stammered.

'Suppose?' She laughed. 'If you suppose, then you haven't.'

I got up feeling angry like, but not knowing why.

'Now don't be like that, Steve,' she said, and took my arm. 'I was only asking a simple question.'

'Well, I dunno then. If that's what you want me to say.' I was getting a distinct whiff of that perfume again. Her hand slid down my arm, and her fingers grasped mine. 'Just take life as it comes,' she whispered.

'I do,' I said. I couldn't tell if she was serious or what. I'd already got my usual hard-on whenever I got within two feet of her. If she started to play silly buggers with me, I wouldn't be responsible for my actions.

Then she put my finger in her mouth, looking at me the while. That was too much. I leant down and kissed her hard. Her wet tongue came out to meet me; this was no shy maiden, that's for sure. We kissed for some time. She was lying on her back, so it was natural for me to get on top of her. She was hot for it all right, and I was out of my mind. I came too quickly while she was still at the early moaning stage. We could hear the guide calling for us.

'Sorry,' I mumbled, doing up my shorts.

'That's all right,' she replied. She hoisted up her knickers, lit a cigarette and said: 'We'd better be getting back to the others.'

'Sorry,' I repeated meself stupidly. I'd messed it up for sure.

She smiled sweetly. 'Don't worry about it. Practice makes perfect.'

The future looked good with that, so we went back to the jeep, and continued our tour.

It was a beautiful island all right, with the south side facing Tahiti, and looking quite different from where we were anchored. We got back to the yacht in time for lunch. Clouds had appeared ever so quick, and it started to rain. Dickie wasn't up to eating, so I went to see him, but he waved me away, saying to enjoy meself and not to worry about him. When people tell you not to worry, it usually means that's when they want you to worry, and I was getting concerned about the old codger. I said so to Eric, but he told me not to worry too.

After lunch, Yolanda said she would be having a nap, and left for her cabin, giving me the come-on as hard as you like. I followed her down after a decent interval, and the afternoon passed very nicely indeed, thank you very much.

MAGGIE

Janet took badly with me going out with Alan. Very badly. She was rude to him, and when she's rude she's very very rude. Poor Alan didn't know what had hit him. It was my fault, of course. I hadn't cleared it with Janet. I don't seem to be very good at managing things at the moment.

Anyway, Janet left the flat ahead of us, slamming the door and running down the stairs without saying goodbye. Oh well.

He asked me where I wanted to go, and I didn't know. Couldn't care less, more like. Full of guilt as usual. So we went to a quiet pub, where he sat me down for a chat. I was wishing I hadn't come. But we had a couple of drinks, and he told me a bit about himself. His parents were both dead, and he had fended for himself more or less since he left school. He did a few odd jobs before he got taken on by a plumber, who taught him the trade but didn't pay him much. He was living with his aunt at the time. Then a couple of years ago, she died and left him the flat he was still living in. It was then he started up on his own. Things were bad at first, but people began to trust him and he became very popular with his customers. He was 28 and working up a nice little business. Now he was wanting to open his own little shop and branch out a bit. girlfriends? There had been one or two, he said, but nothing steady. He'd never really had time for a long-term relationship.

But now – now he was getting heavy – now he was wanting a long-term relationship.

'What'ya mean by long-term?' I asked.

He looked at me long and hard. 'Like forever,' he whispered.

Oh jings. That's all I needed at this stage. I tried to lighten it up a bit. 'Are you proposing marriage, kind sir?' I giggled.

He reddened. Obviously the wrong thing to say. 'Could be,' he muttered.

'Alan,' I began, 'we hardly know each other.' How often do you hear that on the telly? But then I'm not a very original girl.

'I know you well enough to want to know you better,' he muttered again.

There was something very vulnerable about him. There he sat, a good-looking guy if ever there was, building up his own business, yet being gentle and sensitive. I swallowed my wine.

'So what do you say?' he went on. 'Will you give it a chance?'

It was good to be wanted, and so fervently, by a man I didn't know well, but I certainly wanted to know better. 'Where is this flat of yours?' I asked. I didn't think it was the moment to talk about our age difference.

He smiled at me, relieved and pleased. 'Not far. You want to see it?'

Actually I did. We finished our drinks, and he bought a bottle of wine – none of your plonk that Janet and I had been slurping down, but a bottle costing over a tenner .We walked round to his flat, which was further away than I had thought. It was one of those converted houses, with a garden front and back. His was on the ground floor. He held open the door for me to walk in first.

I was stunned. OK, it wasn't enormous or grand or anything like that, but what he had done to it showed taste and imagination. The sitting room had a lavender wallpaper, with rose-coloured velvet curtains and chairs. The carpet echoed the wallpaper and was soft and luxurious to walk on. The kitchen was ultra modern with a greenish tiled floor. The bathroom too was modern, with a new power shower and bathroom suite. The deep blue tiles on the walls and floor gave it a Mediterranean feeling.

'Alan,' I said,' it's absolutely gorgeous. It must have cost you a packet.

'I did most of it myself,' he said. 'At nights. After work.' He took me by the arm. 'And this is the bedroom.'

Again it was unusual, but restful. The carpet was a deep rust colour, with bronze curtains; apple green walls and a bright yellow bedspread.

'This was my aunt's room, which I've moved into,' he explained. 'My old room is smaller, and I haven't done anything with it yet. Dunno what to make it into. A study or something, I suppose.'

This turned out to be a fair size room, but in the need of redecorating. 'Alan, You're fantastic. You're hiding your light under a bushel.'

He opened the wine and we made ourselves cosy on the comfy settee. He told me his plans: how he'd like to go into remaking people's bathrooms and kitchens on a personalised basis. Giving them the best possible for a good price.

I could see he was capable of making a go of it too.

'And I wondered if you'd like to come in with me,' he said blushing again like a schoolboy.

'What'ya mean come in with you?'

'Well. Whatever. You haven't got much a of a job have you at Sainsbury's? Why not help me in the shop and build it up with me?'

I opened my mouth to answer. 'And why not move in here with me, as well?' he ended with a rush.

'Move in?'

He kissed me gently on the mouth and held me close. 'Maggie, let's get to know each other really well. Let's see what's what. What do you say?'

'You mean give up my flat?' I'm a canny Scot and don't like to burn bridges.

'Well, it's not economical is it for us to have two. Wouldn't you like it here?'

'It's not that, Alan. You're just moving a bit fast for me, that's all. I did say to Steve we'd sort it out when he got back, and -'

'Have you decided how you want it sorted?'

'Yes, I think so. It's over.'

He kissed me again, but this time his tongue found its way into me. 'Want to spend the night here with me?' he whispered.

I nodded, feeling better than I'd done for weeks. My life seemed to be taking shape again.

STEVE

The next few days were a bit of a disaster really. We went to Huahine, another island, which was supposed to be fantastic. I wouldn't know. It came on to rain, and it came down in sheets. This went on and on for a couple of days. Everybody said this was most unusual: this wasn't the rainy season. They say that all summer in England too. When it lessened up a bit, we managed to get off the bloody boat for a while, but it wasn't much fun. Evidently there were some fabulous beaches and snorkelling and that, but the rain never let up enough for us to get going. I could have been in Dover.

Most of the time we were all stuck together on the yacht, which seemed to get smaller and smaller every day. Dickie was still not well: he said he had a bad headache - a migraine - and didn't want to talk much. I looked in on him now and then, but he told me to go and enjoy myself. Fat chance. I was getting real worried about him, and suggested we get a doctor, but he wouldn't hear of it. Eric was no barrel of laughs either. The rain wasn't helping his old bones, so he kept himself pretty much to himself.

That left Yolanda. Yolanda - she was one hot piece of woman was Yolanda. I thought I was pretty sexy and that, but she could never get enough of it. Some kind of nympho I reckon. Mind you, she was great in bed, and quite funny out of it. We got on real well together, but our points of conversation were a bit different. I couldn't keep up with all her name-dropping and that, so whenever we got stuck for something to say, she'd stick her tongue down my throat and we'd be in bed again. Very exhausting.

Then we went on to Bora Bora, and as we approached the lagoon, the sun came out at last, and we were back in Paradise. The most beautiful island in the world, some say. I wouldn't argue with that, even though I didn't see much of it. There was this big Mt. Otemanu sticking up with its head in the clouds like a massive tombstone. And then there were these lagoons, so deep and clear. You wanted to dive in the water all the time. We anchored at the Yacht Club, and Eric decided to take us all out to lunch. Dickie was feeling a bit better, so the four of us went ashore in quite high spirits .

The food was great, and I managed to persuade Dickie not to eat any of that delicious seafood as he always seemed to get sick afterwards. He agreed, but he couldn't take his greedy little eyes off my shrimps cooked in a curry sauce. I also managed to keep him off the drink for once, and he agreed to that too, to my surprise. The sun was hot, but we were all relieved to see it, and Yolanda was exposing as much of her flesh as decency would allow.

After lunch, Eric said he was going back to his cabin for a doze, and Yolanda was looking at me with eyes full of promise, as the books say. Dickie asked me what I wanted to do that afternoon, and I said I didn't mind.

'What about a trip round the island?'

'Are you sure you're up to it?' I asked.

'Course I am. Go back and get your swimming things and I'll organise a taxi.'

Yolanda was looking disappointed, so Dickie half-heartedly invited her too. I could see she didn't want to be stuck with old Dickie when she said she'd go back with Eric to 'freshen up a little'. She shot me a sympathetic glance as if I was doing a penance. Well, it was my job, and people were tending to forget that. And I felt I'd been letting old Dickie down these last few days. Actually, I was quite happy to go with him. Conversation with him was always interesting, and sometimes stimulating. He knew a thing or two, did Dickie, and I could ask him about surrealism and all.

In the end he hired a car, as it was cheaper and more convenient in the long run. You could hardly get lost in Bora Bora, as the road just went along the shore round the whole island.

So we went to this Sofitel Hotel near Matira Point, which had a fabulous white beach on the blue, blue water. It was mostly quite shallow and sandy, so I had a long swim all over the lagoon, being able to rest now and then, while Dickie sat on the hotel terrace having a pot of tea. I came out of the water feeling great, and didn't bother to towel myself down, but let that sun get to me. Dickie was by the pool under an umbrella with his eyes closed. I lay down beside him on a mattress. Life was great. This could go on forever as far as I was concerned.

RICHARD

I looked at Steve as he lay down beside me, his brown body dripping salt water, his hair all tousled, and his wet swimming trunks outlining his genitalia. My feelings were ambivalent as I gazed. He was the lover I'd never have, and the son I'd always wanted.

It was time I told him.

'Good swim?' I murmured.

He looked up at me. 'Thought you were asleep.' he smiled.

'No. Just dozing, enjoying the day.'

'It's brilliant this place, isn't it?'

'Yes.' I braced myself. 'Steve,' I began.

'Yeah?'

'I've got to tell you something.'

'Oh yeah?'

'Yes. I should have told you before.'

He sat up, looking anxious. 'What's up?' he asked.

'Well, I haven't been strictly honest with you. At least not at the beginning.'

'Whad'ya mean?' he laughed. 'Don't tell me you're not gay. You're a hetero all along.'

'No, nothing like that. It's – well, I've got a brain tumour.'

'Brain tumour?' He looked at me, his face all serious. 'What does that mean?'

'It means I haven't got much longer to live.'

'You wha'?'

'It's called glioma. It's a kind of cancer.'

'Jesus Christ. Can't they do anything? I mean, these days – '

'No, they can't. It was left too late. I mean it was diagnosed too late. If I'd gone to the doctor sooner, perhaps they could have done something. But I just had headaches at the beginning and felt a bit weak. By the time I went, I had left it too late. Too late to operate, I mean.'

'So, how long have you known?'

'Oh, three months or so.'

'Just before you met me?'

'Yes.'

'So you knew when you met me?'

'Yes. I'm sorry, Steve.'

He shifted himself to a sitting position. 'But what I don't understand is why you advertised for a bloke like me. Why didn't you get yourself a proper nurse and that?'

This was the hardest part to explain. 'I didn't want a nurse. I didn't want someone to be at my side all day saying don't do this, don't do that.'

'But why me? I ain't no nurse.'

'I'm not, not ain't.' I couldn't stop that coming out. To my surprise, he grinned.

'Sorry. I am trying, you know.'

'I know. You're doing wonders.'

'So why me? I'm not a nurse.'

'No. Well, yes you are. The best nurse I could have wished for, actually.'

'I don't get it.'

'No, I'm sure you don't. When they told me I probably had a short time to live, I realised I wanted to live it to the full. I wanted to go mad. I wanted to do all sorts of things. But not alone. I didn't want to be alone. I wanted to spend my last days with someone I -' I stopped.

'With a bloke like me, you mean?'

'Well, yes in a way. I wanted to be with someone who made me feel alive, not some starched old nurse.'

'Some nurses are quite sexy,' he started, then realised. 'Sorry. I mean to me they are. Not male ones of course.'

'Someone who gave me a kick out of life,' I finished.

'I do that?' He was astonished.

'Yes, of course you do. But you know that.'

'Not really. Some times you look as if I piss you off. I'm always saying the wrong thing.'

'Never, Steve. Well, maybe at the beginning, but not recently. Not now.'

'Well, I dunno what to say. I mean, how long – I mean, it sounds a bit heartless, don't it? How long have you got?'

'Doesn't it, not don't it. And it's not heartless. You of all people have a right to know. And the answer is, I don't know. It could be weeks, or a month or two. Or I could be the exception and last for years yet. But I'm not a young man, so the odds are weeks.'

'Well, you never know -' he began.

'I think I do,' I said. 'I've been feeling worse lately. I'm vomiting more. My headaches are becoming more frequent, and my muscles are like jelly sometimes. '

'So it wasn't food poisoning you had, even in India?'

'No. Vomiting is one of the symptoms, I'm afraid. I'm sorry, Steve.'

'Don't see why you should be sorry. It's me that's sorry about you and all.'

'I took you on under false pretences. I deliberately led you into thinking this would be permanent. And as you can see, it won't be. I'm sorry.'

'Oh yeah. Well, forget it, mate.'

'I also want to apologise for putting you into danger.'

'Danger?'

'Yes. Making you smuggle things through Customs. It was an outrageous thing for me to do.'

'I got a buzz from it.'

'I know you did, and that makes me feel even more guilty. I was doing those things because I couldn't care less. It didn't matter to me whether I was caught or not. Why should I care? But you. It could have ruined you for life.'

'Yeah, well.'

'But I will say this. If we or you had been caught, I would have taken full responsibility, I swear to you I would.'

'Yeah, I'm sure you would, Dickie. It's no big deal, mate.'

'Yes, it is. Mate.' And we both smiled at each other. 'You forgive me?'

'Yeah. Sure.' He turned and looked out at the lagoon. 'So what happens now?'

'I don't know, Steve. It's up to you. I don't suppose you want to stay with a dying man. You've got our own life to live.'

'Well, as you say, you may last for years yet.' He looked at me and grinned cheerily. 'And don't forget, mate, we're all going to die some time or other. I may go before you, you never know.'

I could have hugged him when he said that: always the optimist. 'You've answered your own question by saying that,' I said. 'That's the reason I wanted someone like you. You always cheer me up.'

His smile faded. 'Yeah,' he said. 'But who's to cheer me up?'

'I'll do my best. But it's not a very good one.'

'Yeah. Well, there you go.'

We fell silent after that, gazing out at that deep blue lagoon, each with our own thoughts. Neither of us felt like going round the island any more, so we stayed where we were until it was time to return to the yacht.

I asked Steve not to say anything to Eric. He was in bad enough shape himself, without him thinking he had to be concerned about me.

STEVE

Dinner was supposed to be a festive occasion, as it was our last night on the yacht. But after what Dickie told me, and the way he was looking, it took me all my time to behave in me usual cheery fashion. Eric didn't seem to notice, but Yolanda was giving me strange looks. There was the usual champagne and toasts and all, but the evening fell flat as a crab's arse. Dickie excused himself as soon as he could, and went below to his cabin. Yolanda also went below to do one of her freshening up acts, so Eric and I were left alone for a few minutes.

'She seems to have taken quite a fancy to you,' Eric said, watching Yolanda 's bum waggling down the stairs.

'Yeah,' was all I could manage.

'So what are your plans?'

'Plans?' I looked at him stupidly. 'We're leaving tomorrow for Fiji. You know that.'

'You really want to go?'

'Whad'ya mean?'

'I mean if you like, you're welcome to continue the cruise with us for a while. We'd be glad to have you.'

'Oh. Yeah. Well. I work for Dickie, you know.'

'Yes, I know. He's none too well, is he?'

'You reckon?'

'I reckon. He's no spring chicken. Neither of us are. "Gather ye rosebuds while ye may" is my motto in life.'

'Yeah. Well.' I was feeling right uncomfortable here. It's true I'd been thinking a lot about what I was going to do when Dickie died like, but I couldn't see clearly that far ahead. Take life as it comes, everybody says. How would Dickie feel if I left him right now? It'd be more than cruel. I couldn't do that to the old codger. I don't think I even wanted to. On the other hand, was he expecting me to live with him and nurse him and that? Don't think I'm up to that.

'Kind of you,' I said to Eric, 'but I've got to stay with Dickie. He's my employer after all.'

Eric patted me on the shoulder. 'You do what you think is best, Steve. But remember, it's your life – and for God's sake live it to the full. It's over soon enough, you'll see.'

Actually, he was quite a decent old codger, was Eric. I had come to see his good points. When I first met him, I thought he fancied me. I dunno – I must be getting conceited. But when I mentioned this to Dickie, he was horrified, and gave me long accounts of what Eric got up to when he was young and all.

Yolanda returned all freshened up and ready for a night of it. 'Perhaps you can persuade him,' Eric smiled at her. 'I'm off to my bed too.'

We said goodnight, and Yolanda sat down next to me drenched in perfume. 'So, my tough guy, what have you decided to do?'

'I told Eric,' I replied. 'Leave with Dickie tomorrow for Fiji.'

'Please yourself,' she pouted. 'But what do you want to stay with him for?'

' 'Cos he's my boss for one thing.'

'Not much future in that,' she said.

'And what future would I have here then?'

'Well, we could see about that. You could do well for yourself.'

'How?'

'Stay with me and you'll find out.' She took my hand in hers and sucked my middle finger. 'You like that, don't you? Makes you think of what you're going to do next.'

Unfortunately, she was right. We went down to her cabin, and shagged ourselves rotten all night.

Early next morning, I helped Dickie with his packing. He was looking a bit better; thank goodness, because we had a long wait in Papeete before catching the flight to Fiji, which left in the middle of the night. Dickie wasn't looking forward to it one bit. He was annoyed because the last time he did the journey, there was a flight in the afternoon, but now everything left during the night.

Eric and Yolanda came with us to Bora airport to see us off. Dickie was quite tearful saying goodbye to Eric; it was obvious he thought he would never see him again. I sighed inwardly. Life was going to be ever so morbid in the months ahead. Yolanda gave me a long wet kiss in front of Dickie – I think she did it deliberately. It certainly upset him. I saw his eyes watching me nervously.

'I'm going to miss you,' she whispered in my ear. 'I like a bit of rough.'

That was it then. That's all I was to her. How far would I have got with a woman like that? She'd throw me aside the minute she got bored with me. I said good bye to her politely, thinking she was in for a right boring cruise with Eric unless she found a native or two to give her one.

It started to rain as we boarded the tiny plane, so visibility was too poor to say a proper goodbye to Bora Bora. Still, at least I'd seen it. Not many back home had done that.

We spent the rest of the day in the Hotel Tahiti. It rained on and off most of the time, so when we boarded the flight to Fiji, Dickie was definitely the worse for wear. He even refused the welcoming aboard champagne, and fell asleep the moment the plane took off. I tried to sleep but couldn't, thinking about my future – or lack of it, more like. The more I thought of it, the more I realised that Dickie had landed me in the shit. He had promised a permanent job, though to be fair, I suppose I haven't wasted all that much time, and there isn't much doing anyway. But after all our gallivanting and that, it's going to be hard settling down to life again in Ashford. There's Maggie of course: I'd be able to give her more time, if I haven't left it too late. I certainly didn't fancy living with Dickie in that big empty house with him getting sicker and sicker all the time. I hate illness I do, and I certainly ain't no wet nurse. (I find Dickie's 'double negative' very satisfying in moments of stress – like swearing. Can't understand why there's a law against it.) Anyway, I'll just have to get through this trip with him, and see how it goes.

We got to the Regent Hotel in Fiji about breakfast time, but Dickie wanted to go straight to bed. I helped him to his room and that, before going down to get a good meal. The beach was nice, except it was black sand, so I lay me down on a sun bed and got in some serious tanning. Later I took the hotel boat to the hotel's private island a few miles off shore. The swimming was good from there so the day passed pleasantly enough, and the sun and sea had raised my spirits again. Life would be all right, I said to meself, provided I took the right road. Whatever that meant. (I don't half have some silly thoughts sometimes.)

The Regent was some hotel all right. Evidently it was supposed to be the best in the South Pacific, and I'd go along with that with my limited experience. The luxurious rooms were scattered about the gardens, so you felt real privacy even though your room was in a block. And the people were right friendly, shouting 'bula' at you all the time and grinning at you like mad. The women were a bit scary though, with their fuzzy hair and built like rugby players: they looked strong enough to beat me up if they felt like it. The men were even bigger, so there was no question of having an argument with those guys. Still, I had good day all round, and when Dickie appeared in the late afternoon he seemed in good spirits too.

'What you been doing all day?' I asked him.

'Sitting on my balcony, enjoying the gardens, and reading. And you?'

I told him about my day, and we sat watching the sun set over the distant islands. Like Moorea, it was another spectacular sight, giving you a sense of awe and that. There was a crash of drums, and this native guy in a grass skirt ran all over the place lighting torches in the semi-darkness.

'Charming,' said Dickie.

'Yeah,' I replied, 'The tom-toms, or whatever, really get you going.'

It grew darker, and the yellow sunset was slowly turning to night, and we sat on in silence with just the flaring torches casting shadows.

Finally Dickie spoke: 'Steve?'

'Yeah?'

'Have you decided, thought of, what you're going to do...after?'

'I dunno,' I said, and left it like that.

RICHARD

I didn't much care for the Blue Lagoon Cruise, but Steve enjoyed it. We left the Regent Hotel mid-morning, and were driven to Lautoka further north, where the cruise would begin. We had to check in by 1.30, but didn't sail until 3 p.m., so I was a bit tetchy with all the hanging around.

The cabins were all right, I suppose, but the ship was full of Australians and New Zealanders. They were friendly enough, but I wasn't up to the childish games after dinner on the deck. I've got beyond the 'one man went to mow' stage. So it was another early night for me.

The next day was brilliant sunshine. We were anchored in a sparkling blue lagoon, the sight of which, I must admit, took one's breath away. We all went ashore and sported ourselves in the water, while the crew prepared a kind of barbecue. Afterwards, Steve and I walked along the white sand away from the rest and sat on the beach looking at the opalescent water.

'Enjoying yourself?' I asked after a while.

'Yeah, it's excellent.' he replied with a grin. 'You feeling better today? You're looking good.'

'Yes, thanks. Today's a good day. I feel fine. I do think the weather and ambience help, don't you?'

He looked puzzled for a moment and then nodded. 'Dickie,' he said, 'Why are we here?'

'What do you mean?'

'Well, we seem to be wandering about for no reason. Aren't you up to anything these days?'

I smiled. 'No, not really. Apart from the pearls I bought in Tahiti. I was furious I was too ill to shop in Moorea – they're cheaper there.'

'And here?'

'In Fiji? There's not much here except duty-frees, and even they're not always a good bargain. We might pick up an opal or two in Nandi before we leave.'

'Then what are we doing?'

'Having a holiday.'

'And that's all?'

'Yes. What more do you want?'

'It's not what I want. Dickie. I'm enjoying it and that, but you said we were going to Samoa.'

'And so we are. After this.'

'I know. But we've taken a helluva time to get there. What's so special about it anyway?'

'It's a nice place, I believe.'

'I'm sure. But that was the whole point of taking me on, wasn't it? To go to Samoa?'

'Partly, yes. But I've enjoyed our travels, haven't you?'

Steve sighed and shook his head. 'You're an irritating old bastard sometimes, Dickie. Come on, man. Why am I always the last to know?'

'You're not the last, Steve. All right, I'll tell you. And for your information, you're the only one to know.'

So I told him. I told him that Samoa was actually two separate states.

One was American Samoa, which, although independent by name, had the presence of the US Department of the Interior; and Western Samoa, a state in its own right, formerly belonging to New Zealand.

'So we're going to Western Samoa, right?' He asked.

'Right,' I replied.

'So, why?'

'Why? Because that's where Philip died.'

Steve whistled at that. 'Your – guy? What was he doing there?'

'On a day trip from American Samoa. He was working there for the Government, and went over to Western Samoa for the day with Hilary.'

'His wife?'

'Yes. They'd taken a taxi up to Vailima, where Robert Louis Stevenson's house was. You knew he died there?'

'Who Stevenson? No, I don't think so.'

'Well, he built a house half way up from the town and lived there for the last few years of his life. Philip wanted to see it, as he was a great fan. He loved *Dr Jekyll and Mr Hyde*.'

'Oh yeah,' Steve had registered the name at last. 'It was a great film. Several films actually. Yeah, that was Stevenson.'

'And *Treasure Island*, and *Kidnapped*, 'I added tactfully. 'Anyway, Philip was a bit of a Jekyll and Hyde himself, so probably that's why he liked the story. So they trekked up to the top to look at his grave. It was very hot and humid that day evidently, and they were thankful to get back to Stevenson's house. They were sitting by the bathing pool that Stevenson had built in the rocks when Philip – he – Philip had a heart attack. Hilary ran back to the house and they got him to the hospital, but he died that evening.'

'God. So you want to see his grave then?'

'No, Steve. Just where he died. The US Government flew his body back to the States, and he was buried in the family plot in San Francisco.'

'Which is where we're going after that. Now you tell me. Why so secretive?'

'I don't know. I suppose it's just such a secret part of my life. I didn't – don't want people to know. You're the only person I've told.'

Steve took my hand and grasped it tight. 'You're a silly old bugger, Dickie. You know that?'

That was one of the most beautiful moments of my life after Philip. Looking out at that peaceful paradise, with my hand in his, even if it were only for a moment.

We returned to the group and then back to the ship. It was only a three-night cruise, but Steve managed to latch on to some New Zealand girl with the most atrocious vowels I've ever heard. Just how far he got with her I never did find out. I didn't dare ask him outright as I didn't want to handle the answer: I was still far too possessive and jealous. But the cruise ended at last, and we got back to Lautoka in the middle of the afternoon, where we returned to the Regent for one night before going onto Samoa.

STEVE

I liked Fiji: the people were great, likewise the scenery, and that mini-cruise was fun. There was this New Zealand girl who chatted me up, or was it the other way round? Anyway, her dragon mother never left her side, so it was difficult to gain entry, so to speak. She had the fancy name of Clarissa, and was a bit old-fashioned in her outlook, but sexy in a puritanical sort of way. We had a few chats after Dickie went to bed, and mother had a problem keeping her eyes open, but in the end when she went to bed, Clarissa always went with her. They were staying at the Regent too, so I saw them again the evening we returned from the cruise. Dickie and me were having dinner by the pool, and Clarissa and Mum were munching away on the other side. She gave me the eye right enough when her mother was deep in the trough, and a few winks to go with it. Dickie caught one of them, and didn't look best pleased about it for some reason. When we'd finished, he asked me to check what time our flight left the next day and get the bill.

He'd settle it in the morning. We sat for a while watching some Fiji dancing, and then he said goodnight, and went off to his room. I was left to my own devices, and wandered along the tree-fringed beach for a bit under the flaming torches Clarissa appeared from nowhere, and we started chatting. Mother had the runs evidently and had to give up the chaperone bit.

She took my arm and squeezed it, so I didn't think there was much need for more conversation. I put my arms round her and kissed her chastely on the lips. It was chaste 'cos her lips remained rock solid. I was patient for a bit, then tried a second offensive, but the portcullis stayed down.

'What's the matter?' I asked. 'Don't you like it?'

'Oh yes,' she replied. 'It's just I think you're rushing it a bit.'

Rushing it? This was Fiji, at the end of the twentieth century, for God's sake. 'How old are you?' I asked.

'Twenty-six,' she replied, lowering her eyes modestly.

Christ, a professional virgin. Waiting for Mr Right, no doubt. Why her mother thought she needed a chaperone was one of life's mysteries; she needed a randy girlfriend to help get her going more like.

'I expect you think I'm a bit old-fashioned,' she said. 'And I suppose I am. I'm just waiting for Mr Right to come along.'

'Yeah,' I said, as politely as I could.

We said goodnight soon after, and I left her outside her block under the palms. I strolled back to Reception and got the bill sorted out, and rechecked our departure time from the hotel. It was still early, so I decided to take it to Dickie's room and leave it under his door.

Like all the accommodation in the hotel, the rooms were on two floors in blocks scattered about the gardens. I climbed the wooden stairs and found his room number. I was just bending down with the bill, when I heard voices inside. Who on earth could he be talking to? Then I heard a cry. That was definitely Dickie, and he was in trouble again. I banged loudly on the door. 'Dickie,' I shouted. 'Are you all right?'

The voices stopped, then Dickie's quavering voice called out: 'Is that you, Steve? Come in, please.'

I tried the door, but it was locked. 'Open the door then, Dickie,' I shouted. 'D'ya want me to break it down?' A bit difficult that would be. It was solid.

A scuffling sound and the key was turning in the lock. To my surprise, a huge Fijian opened the door, and smiled at me. 'Bula,' he said, and let me in.

'Bula to you too,' I replied, and went over to the bed where Dickie was lying, as a white as the sheet he was pulling over himself. 'What the hell's going on?' I said.

Dickie took my hand and held it tight. 'Sorry, Steve,' he said. 'Sorry.'

'For what?' I asked, still puzzled. I looked around but the Fijian had scarpered. I could hear his bare feet padding down the wooden stairs. I shut the door. 'What are you up to, Dickie?'

He was shuddering as if he was cold. 'Pour me a whisky, there's a good lad.' I poured him a stiff one and put it in his hands. They were shaking.

'Sorry, Steve, sorry,' he said again.

'So tell me.'

'I know I'm stupid. Don't think bad of me, Steve. I couldn't help it.'

'What for God's sake? What were you doing with that giant?'

'What it looks like. Having sex.'

My mouth opened wide. 'You wha' – ?'

'Yes, well,' he said. 'Everyone's having a good time, aren't they? Everyone was having fun on the cruise, weren't they? And you with that girl with the vowels.'

'What vowels – ?'

'And Rana before that. What about me? Why shouldn't I have fun too?'

I couldn't answer that, though I must say I was bit shocked, and I didn't think I was the shockable sort. 'So you picked him up, did you?'

'Not exactly,' he said, swigging his whisky down. 'I think he's a night porter or something. Anyway, he was on this floor when I came up the stairs and asked me if I wanted anything. And it wasn't a straight question either, Steve. He definitely gave me the double meaning look. So I smiled and asked if he could bring me some ice. Which he did. He then asked if there was anything more, and the conversation took off from there. You know how it is.'

I do, actually.

'I'm not a fool, Steve. I knew he wasn't lusting after my body, so I asked him how much he wanted. He gave an equivocal reply, but by then I was past caring. I undressed and lay on the bed. He came over and started to – well, you know – '

Tell me about it. Presumably foreplay is the same whatever sex you're into.

'Then he said he liked my watch, and asked to try it on. I refused. And he got a bit rough. 'What you give me then?' he shouted. 'Where's your wallet?' Things were getting rather nasty when, thank God, you came along. God knows what might have happened.'

I looked at him – the poor old, lonely man – and felt so sorry for him; so intensely sorry for this guy who had loved someone so deeply and then spent the rest of his life alone. Who was I to criticise? God, he had found love, felt that deep emotion for another human being, and I hadn't. I realised I'd never been in love. It was always sex with me first and last. I felt affection maybe. Fondness even. But love? I don't think so. Not even with Maggie. I'd been kidding myself and her all along. I liked her a lot, she was a good mate, but I didn't love her. Suddenly I felt frightened: here I was at thirty-five, and never had a serious relationship with anyone. And look at dear old Dickie – ashamed of himself for feeling desperate and doing what I would be doing meself at his age, then boasting to me mates I could still get it up and all.

I took the empty whisky glass form his hand and put it on the table. I took his hand in both of mine and said: 'I told you once before, Dickie me lad. You're a silly old bugger and no mistake. But don't you ever apologise to me again for nothing. Understand?'

His red eyes looked up at me as he held my hand. He blinked to keep the tears away, then let go my hand, and smiled. 'Thanks – even if it was a double negative.'

I got up to refill his glass. 'I know Dickie, me boy. I know. You and your grammar. That much you have taught me.'

I sat by his bed for a while, and drank a whisky with him.

RICHARD

I felt very foolish the next morning; I was worried how Steve would react in the clear light of day, but he breezed into the dining room in his usual cheery fashion and sat down opposite. I gave him a hesitant smile. 'Morning,' I said.

'And how's the old sexpot today then?' He grinned at me.

I felt my face reddening. 'Thoroughly ashamed of myself,' I muttered.

'Why?' he said. 'You should be thankful you can still do it. Most guys would give their right testicle to do what you can do. Although, I suppose, if they gave their right testicle then they wouldn't be able to do nothing.'

I had to smile. 'And don't tell me about double negatives again, all right?' he went on. 'I've got the hang of them now. But sometimes they're more effective than your proper grammar.' He waved to the waitress, and ordered a huge breakfast. She smiled at him and poured some coffee.

'Tell you one thing, Dickie me lad. I'm a bit disappointed with the dusky maidens bit. They're all built like King Kong and definitely on the make.'

We flew to Western Samoa in the afternoon, and were driven to the main town of Apia. Apia is in fact the only town, and can hardly be called a town at that. It's just a collection of buildings. It was hot and humid, so we arranged ourselves by the pool in Aggie Grey's Hotel, and spent the rest of the day sunning ourselves and having a gentle swim. I told Steve he could go into town if he wanted, but he didn't seem to want to leave me. I must say I was much comforted by his solicitude.

We had dinner that evening in the hotel and watched the usual song and dance show afterwards. I quite enjoy the South Seas music and rhythm. In that climate, it is most seductive - unfortunately for me.

I was going up to Vailima tomorrow morning, and Steve wanted to know if he was coming too. I was in two minds about this. I wanted to be alone at the time, but on the other hand, he was now the only person who knew why I was going, and might be of help if I were taken ill.

'D'you mind coming with me to the house, and then we'll decide after that?' I asked.

'Sure,' he nodded. 'Whatever you say. I'll just hang out and wait for orders.'

The next morning we took a taxi after breakfast to Vailima to begin my pilgrimage. Stevenson's house was built in colonial style with a veranda running round the ground and upper story. There were trees at the back, but the front had been cleared to make a kind of tropical lawn, so that the sea could be glimpsed through the trees in the hazy distance. It was still hot and humid as we inspected the house, before making our way to the swimming pool that Stevenson had built. Mt. Vaea loomed overhead, its peak surrounded in cloud. There was a notice pointing to the trail to the top, where Stevenson was buried. I asked Steve if he minded leaving me here, and he nodded understandingly, and said he would climb up and look at the tomb.

It was still fairly early, and the tourists had not yet arrived. It was very quiet as I picked my way down the path to the watering hole hewn out of the rocks, with a miniature cascade trickling into the cool water. It was one of the most peaceful and evocative spots I have ever visited. There were ferns and shrubs under the trees, and I thought of the joy and relief Stevenson must have felt in that silent - almost holy - place. It was holy to me, of course, because this was where my beloved Philip had rested after coming down from the top of Mt. Vaea. I could see the ledge where he probably sat with Hilary, trying to recover from the climb. And then the heart attack. I imagined Hilary, frightened out of her wits, trying to help him, then running and sliding up the slippery path to get help from the house. Oh, Philip, my dear Philip. If only I had been there to comfort you – although there was nothing more that I could have done. But just to be with you in your last moments. The ambulance arriving, the race to the hospital, and then – you died in Hilary's arms. Oh, Philip, my dear. How I loved you. I'll always love you, my darling, to the end of my days.

I broke down then, and cried my eyes out. The still air hugged me close, and I could almost feel him holding me the way he used to. I lay down on the ledge and prayed. I don't believe in God, or life after death, but still I prayed. To whom and for what I can't remember, but I stopped crying and felt a kind of calm.

Steve came back after a long time. He looked at me with concern. 'All right, mate?' He asked.

'Yes. Yes, I think so,' I replied.

'D'ya want to stay a while longer?'

I shook my head. 'No, thanks. Let's go. I've done here.'

He took my arm and helped me up the path and then on to the road down to Apia. We flagged down a passing taxi and returned to the hotel.

But the strain of that journey through the past took its toll, and I had to take to my bed in the afternoon. Steve went for a walk around Apia, but didn't seem much impressed. Next morning we flew to American Samoa for the day, but I was to be disappointed there. It rained steadily, and I searched in vain for the office where Philip had worked. We found Government House all right, but were denied access. It was a frustrating and depressing day altogether. The streets were cemented; there were modern buildings and traffic everywhere. The place was so Americanised we couldn't wait to get out of it and back to Apia. Steve hated it, too, I was glad to see.

The next day we took a trip round the island, but I found it difficult to relax and enjoy myself. I was a bit of a wet blanket, I'm afraid, with the rest of the group. Steve was enjoying himself, but pretending not to in case I would be offended. Dear boy. We did have an enchanting stop near Lalomanu on the south east corner of the island. There was a small island offshore, which had been a leper colony evidently, and we swam in emerald green water off the white sandy shore. Even I felt brighter after a delightful picnic lunch. Further on there was a magnificent waterfall plunging into the green forest below. 'Awesome,' Steve pronounced it.

Still, I was glad to get back to the comfort of Aggie Grey's. We had a gruelling journey the next day to Honolulu and then Los Angeles.

STEVE

I didn't think much of Honolulu. All that hype about Waikiki Beach and that. There were thousands of hotels lining the beach, which was covered with tourists – most of them Japs. The swimming was none too good either. The dusky maidens were very Americanised, so it wasn't much of a tropical paradise except for the weather. We were both knackered after the five-hour flight from Apia, which had left before dawn, so Dickie went straight to bed after a sandwich. Our body clocks weren't in good nick neither, so we were never sure if we were hungry or not. I spent the afternoon wandering along this beach then back to the hotel pool, which was packed with Americans. We both had an early night.

Next day we did a tour of the island, which was all right, but after the South Seas bit, it didn't hold a candle. I liked the beach where they filmed *From Here To Eternity* though, except it wasn't empty as it was in Burt Lancaster's day, but solid with tourists.

Dickie was looking very strained. What he called his pilgrimage in Apia had done him good – he'd come back as if a weight had been lifted, and I'd hopes he'd be his old self again. But the early morning flight, together with the thought of another early morning start the next day, had shattered him. Here's hoping he'll be better when we get to the States.

I tried to phone Maggie. I couldn't work out what time it was in England, so asked at Reception. They were a bit cool, so I took a chance and rang anyway.

A sleepy voice answered. 'Hi, is that you Maggie?' I said brightly.

'Who – is that you Steve?'

'Yeah. Who else?'

'It's awfie early to be calling. Where are you?'

'Still in bed then?'

'Course I'm in bed, you daftie. It's the middle of the night.'

'Sorry.'

'What'ya want?'

This was not going well. 'Thought I'd give you a buzz, that's all. To see how you were.'

'Well, I'm -'

'Who's that?' I heard this man's voice.

'Who's that?' I said, sniffing trouble.

'That's what he just said,' Maggie answered.

'Who?'

'Alan, of course.'

'Alan? Alan who?'

'You know damn well who. Alan Mackay. The plumber.'

'What the hell's the plumber doing in our flat in the middle of the night?'

'He's in bed with me, of course. What'ya think?'

'You wha'...?'

'Steve, I think you've forgotten something. We've split up, or didn't you notice? I'm moving on.'

I was stunned. I hadn't been gone for five minutes and there she was in bed with the plumber. 'Well this is news to me.'

'That's 'cos you don't listen,' Maggie said calmly. 'You're too taken up with yoursell.'

'I am not. I've been thinking of you a lot.'

That wasn't strictly true. I did think of her on and off, but not on a regular basis. My feelings were mixed too: there was a bit of relief creeping in. On the other hand, I was furious she was being unfaithful to me so quickly. 'And I suppose when I come home, he'll still be in my bed?' I said, all hurt, like. I had rights too.

'No, he won't,' she replied calmly. 'As a matter of fact, you were lucky to catch us in. I'm going to live with him in his nice new flat. He only came round to help me pack and clear things out. What with one thing and another it got late, so we stayed the night here instead of there.'

I was speechless. 'Well, of all the...'

'Don't start getting self-righteous with me, Steve Jackman. You've got a brass neck, the way you've been acting.'

'So,' I said with all the dignity I could find, 'When I get home you won't be there?'

'That's right. I'm glad you phoned though, ''cos I was going to have to leave you a note, but it's better to tell you on the phone. Are you enjoying yourself?'

'That's not the point. How can you walk out like that?'

'Don't me daft, Steve. We both knew it was over, but didnae have the courage to make the final break. I'm doing you a favour.'

'Oh, thanks very much.'

'Don't be like that. We'll still be friends. Let me know when you're coming back and I'll get some bread and milk in for you.'

God, women are awesome at times. Bread and milk, for Christ's sake.

'So how's it going?'

I didn't want to talk about it. I wanted to think. So I just said things were all right, but Dickie wasn't too well.

'Sorry to hear that,' she said. 'See you soon then.'

'Yeah.' I slammed the phone down with a clatter, the way they do in films. I never knew how satisfying that was. But I was right pissed off, and told Dickie about it over dinner. He was sympathetic but didn't overdo it. His speech was a bit slurred, though I hadn't seen him drinking much. He looked dead tired. We said goodnight early and went to our rooms to try and catch a bit of sleep before getting up again to catch the early morning flight to L.A.

CHAPTER SEVEN

RICHARD

The flight nearly killed me: I can't be doing with all these time changes and middle of the night flights. By the time we got to LA I was absolutely exhausted, and we still hadn't arrived; but we caught the shuttle to San Francisco fairly easily and got to our hotel in Union Square in the early evening. I took to my bed, while Steve went out to see a bit of the town.

We had an early dinner in my room, then I said goodnight to Steve about ten o'clock. I had a big emotional day coming up: I had phoned Hilary, not expecting her to want to see me, but to my surprise she asked me up to her apartment on Nob Hill for coffee at eleven. People who live in that area don't normally ask but command, so I changed my plans and arranged to go to Philip's grave in the afternoon. I thought it more diplomatic if I saw her alone – I had no idea if she had changed her opinion of 'abnormal deviants', and didn't want to embarrass her or myself – or Steve, for that matter.

So he set off happily for a tour of Alcatraz.

'Why on earth do you want to go there?' I asked.

'It's all them – those – films I've seen. Clint Eastwood and that. I'll bring you back some pictures.'

I can't understand people's morbid interest in such a place, but he waxed enthusiastic like a boy going to Disneyland. He left soon after breakfast, promising to be back by lunchtime to accompany me to the cemetery.

I set off for Nob Hill by taxi, arriving promptly at her door at eleven o'clock. An old black retainer ushered me into the over-furnished but elegant drawing room to await the arrival of Hilary Hansworth. Although the room was spotless and full of light, there was an atmosphere of dust and decay. I had the impression it was used only for visitors – and that there hadn't been many of them in the last few years. It was the house of a lonely old woman. I should know: I expect my house has the aura of a lonely old man. The large picture windows looked over the city to the Bay, and I could make out the island of Alcatraz sparkling in the sun. I thought of Steve happily tramping along the gloomy prison corridors, making that dismal place lively with his cheerful personality, and wished I was with him instead of in this dead monument to the past. There were photographs everywhere; and it wasn't until I looked closer that I realised they were all of Philip with or without Hilary. But the focus was on a huge wedding photo of them in a silver frame on the grand piano. Once aware of it, the photo dominated the room – obviously the intention of the owner.

There was a rustle of silk, and I turned round to see her enter the room leaning heavily on a stick. 'Mr Grayson,' she said, offering her left hand. It was a statement, not a welcome.

I shook it gently, noting the formal greeting, which implied I would have to address her as Mrs Hansworth invoking Philip's surname as her right, and not mine.

'Do sit down,' she waved me to an uncomfortable chesterfield while she seated herself on a high-backed wing chair. She had aged, of course, as we all do, but I was not prepared for such a change. The only time I had met her was when she was young, and she had struck me as a handsome young lady, impeccably dressed in the clothes of the time. Her face was the colour of marble, her sharp nose and chin accentuated by the crimped blue-white hair. Her lavender silk dress was expensive, but dated. In fact, her whole appearance struck me as being mothballed in another age – the age of her youth with Philip. The sparkle on her fingers drew my attention to her hands: they were covered with diamonds and one enormous sapphire. I smiled to myself when I saw that: I could hear Steve saying 'If that ain't a Kashmir blue, then I'll eat my hat.'

'You're smiling, Mr Grayson?' She raised her eyebrows.

I took my eyes away from those hands – unexpectedly large, like a navvy's hands. 'I was thinking of an experience I had in India,' I replied stupidly.

Her lips went hard. 'You travel a lot, I take it.'

This was going to be a difficult interview, and I wondered why she had consented to see me. The frosty atmosphere was broken by the arrival of the retainer carrying an enormous silver tray, which he set down with difficulty in front of her. The whole ambience of her house took me back thirty years; in fact she would have looked slightly out of date even then.

She poured the coffee elegantly, the rings flashing as her big hands manipulated the pot and cups. Perhaps she thought all those rings on her fingers would cover up her unattractive hands, when they in fact accentuated them.

'Yet you have never come to California before,' she said continuing from her previous remark.

'No, never.'

'Strange,' she said, handing me my cup and looking directly into my eyes for the first time. 'You travel all over the world, but don't honour the San Franciscans with a visit. Why should that be, I wonder?'

She bloody well knew why, the old cow. 'I should have thought the reason was obvious, Mrs Hansworth,' I replied coldly. 'Philip is buried here, and I had no desire to revive memories.'

There was a sharp intake of breath. 'Then why now, Mr Grayson?'

'Because I haven't long to live, Mrs Hansworth, that's why. When one knows one's end is near, things take on a different perspective.' No comment. No sign of sympathy. 'I wanted to tidy up the loose ends, as it were, and make the pilgrimage...'

'Pilgrimage?'

'Pilgrimage to Samoa, and then here.'

She looked at me in astonishment. 'You went to Samoa?'

'Yes, I've just been there. We went to Stevenson's house first and – '

'We?' she broke in. 'Who is we?'

Dammit. I hadn't wished to bring up Steve's name. 'My companion,' I explained. 'I need someone to look after me.'

'I see,' she said. 'A nurse then?'

'A bit of both,' I answered weakly.

She drew back in distaste, obviously imagining all sorts of shenanigans. If only, I thought.

'And what did you see in Samoa?'

'The swimming hole where Philip had his heart attack. A very peaceful place. It was difficult to imagine a tragedy occurring there.'

Her eyes softened while she took a sip of her coffee. 'I shall never forget that day,' she said gently. 'Never.'

' I can imagine,' I said. 'It must have been awful for you.'

She looked at me, surprised at my sympathy. 'Yes, it was,' she said. 'A nightmare from which I never really recovered.'

'Were you completely alone?'

'Yes. Just the two of us. It was such a romantic spot.'

She was going to rub it in then.

'We were sitting quietly side by side, watching that little cascade pouring its clear water into the pool, when he suddenly gave a sigh and collapsed in my arms.'

'It was completely unexpected then?'

'Of course. He was a heavy smoker,' she told me, as if I didn't know. 'But we all were in those days, weren't we? He had complained of chest pains, but thought it was indigestion, change of diet, you know.'

Why hadn't he seen a doctor, for God's sake?

'We had climbed to the top to see Stevenson's grave, and he was very out of breath. But we rested a while before commencing the climb down. It was late afternoon, and although we were in the shade, he was sweating profusely. It was at the water hole that the pains got worse, and his face had taken on a shocking blue colour, as if he were cold – but of course it wasn't that at all. Then suddenly he was gone.'

'You got him to hospital?'

'Yes, but I didn't think much of that. Not the same standard as our American ones, you understand. But they did their best. He died almost immediately.'

'Did he say anything?'

'He never regained consciousness. He just slipped away.'

No dying message then. How I had hoped there had been something.

'So I never had the chance to say goodbye to him,' she said softly.

And you think I had? I thought to myself savagely. Could she not see I had grieved – was grieving – as well?

We sat in silence for a moment.

'I don't suppose the place has changed much in all these years?' she said, half in question.

'You never went back then?'

'No, of course not. Sentimental journeys are not my style.'

One in the eye for me then; I turned the other cheek. 'I shouldn't think it has changed,' I replied. 'As I said, it struck me as one of the most peaceful places I have ever visited.'

She nodded, but did not reply for a moment. Then: 'More coffee?' She offered politely as a signal that the interview was over and it was time for me to go.

I declined equally politely, saying I had things to do before visiting his grave that afternoon.

'You're going to Philip's grave?'

'Yes,' I said. 'This afternoon.'

'Do you know where it is?'

'In Oakland, I believe. I have the exact address at the hotel.'

'Where are you staying?' she asked.

'The Prescott, Union Square,' I replied.

She hesitated a moment. 'Philip's grave may not be so easy to find as you think,' she said. 'Why not go in my car? Edward, my chauffeur, knows the way so well. We go every week, you see.'

I was flabbergasted. 'How kind of you, Mrs Hansworth, but I don't wish to cause you any trouble -'

'No trouble at all,' she said, with an imperious wave of her arm. 'Shall we say two o'clock outside your hotel? The car will be waiting.'

'Too kind,' I muttered, as she got to her feet and held out her hand. I wondered if she expected me to kiss it or shake it. I decided on the latter. She walked me slowly to her front door. I protested there was no need, but she insisted. She hesitated for an instant as if there were something else she wished to say; apparently she thought better of it because she took my hand again and said: 'Goodbye, Mr Grayson. It is good of you to visit an old friend's grave.'

So she wasn't admitting it – even after all these years she wouldn't face up to her husband's other love. 'Goodbye,' I said, and walked out into the brilliant sunshine.

I was glad to see Steve waiting for me in the lobby as I entered the hotel. He was full of his trip, but tried hard to look interested in what I had to tell him.

'Sounds a right old bag to me,' he summed it up nicely.

'Yes,' I replied. 'And yet I feel a little sorry for her. Her life hasn't been a happy one, I think.'

'Whose has?' replied Steve, with a grin. 'Pity you missed Alcatraz. It was great, man. Just as I had imagined it.'

'Good,' I said, not in the mood to hear about life in prison. At times one's life seems to be a prison: I'm sure Hilary Hansworth would agree with me on that score.

I told him we were getting a lift in 'the old bag's car', which cheered him up. I imagine he thought the afternoon would be gruesome enough with dreary old me in a cemetery. We had a light snack and waited in the lobby for the car to arrive, which it did on the dot.

The driver, Edward, turned out to be a dishy hunk of a man, and Steve was prompted to ask in a loud whisper if there was something going on in Nob Hill. He carried on in that vein for a while, making more and more outrageous remarks until I laughed out loud. I'm not sure what Edward made of all this, accustomed as he must have been to funereal journeys.

We drove over the Bay Bridge to Oakland, and soon reached the Mountain View Cemetery. Edward and Steve waited by the car while I made my way through a grove of trees to the grave that Edward had pointed out to me. It was a modest, plain tomb – nothing like I had imagined all these years. There was a marble surround and headstone with the words:

Philip Hansworth

Beloved husband of Hilary

'He was a good man, and just.'

1920–1966

There were fresh flowers on the grave, a sign of Hilary's weekly visit. I had brought a silly, single red rose, which I laid in the centre under the gravestone. God knows what Hilary would say when she found it the next time she turned up.

I felt strangely detached from the whole scene. Philip wasn't here. There was much more of him in Samoa by that quiet pool. I looked down on the earth that hid his decayed bones from view and whispered: 'Bye, Philip, my darling. You were the only person I ever loved, and I shall miss you till the day I die.'

As I turned away, I thought what a sentimental foolish old man I was. Till the day I die, indeed. That wasn't going to be long now.

I returned to the car where Steve was looking at me anxiously, wondering how to behave and what to say. 'Let's go,' I said to Edward and got in the car. Strange how some of life's long awaited moments turn out to be damp squibs. The whole afternoon had been an anticlimax.

When we arrived at the hotel, Edward held the car door open for us, and I stopped to thank him. He held out his hand, and at first I thought he was waiting for a tip until I saw he was holding a thick cream-coloured envelope. 'Mrs Hansworth told me to give you this, sir, on your return from the cemetery,' he said.

'What is it?'

'I don't know, sir.' He gave a semi-salute, got into the car and drove off.

We walked into the hotel, I tearing the envelope open the while. There was a note with an old black and white snapshot. I stared at it, puzzled for a moment; then I remembered. I turned to Steve. 'Excuse me, Steve,' I said, trying to control my voice, 'I just want to look at this in private.'

He looked concerned. 'You all right?' he asked.

'Yes, fine, thanks. I'll see you later.'

I almost ran to my room in my haste to read the note. I shut the door, sat on the bed and read:

Dear Mr Grayson,

This old photograph was found in Philip's private papers. I thought you may like to have it. It had quite slipped my mind, but your visit prompted me to look for it.

Sincerely,

Hilary Hansworth.

The snapshot was of Philip and me taken by a friend in Green Park in the 1950s. I remember the day well. We'd had an uproarious lunch at the Ritz and were walking through Green Park together when Philip bumped into some American friends of his. They were doing the usual tourist thing, and one of them snapped the two of us walking under the trees. I was almost doubled over with laughter, while Philip was smiling and waggling his finger at me. I turned the snap over and read Philip's writing:

Dickie and I in Green Park 1953

'Don't laugh at my jokes too much!'...

This may have mystified Hilary, who probably thought it fairly innocuous, although she had taken her time sending it. But to me, it was everything. He was quoting a line from our favourite song from the show *Oklahoma!*, where the next line continued, 'People will say we're in love'. He must have written it intending to send me it, but somehow it had got mislaid and then forgotten. I lay on the bed and sobbed my heart out. All these years I had grieved and wept for him, while time had misted over the memory of his love, and doubt had often crept in. It was all so long ago – maybe I had read too much into it; maybe it wasn't the long-lasting affair that I had thought it was.

And now from the past, he had sent me his declaration, and my whole life had been worthwhile after all.

STEVE

Dickie was a changed man when I met him for dinner. He was bright and cheerful – not at all what I had expected after a visit to the cemetery. It must have had something to do with the note Hilary sent him. He told me she had sent an old photo of Philip and him, but wouldn't say more than that. Anyhow, it was good to see him looking so chirpy again. Back on his old form, he ordered champagne and a huge meal.

'Tell me about Alcatraz, Steve. That's been the highlight of the whole trip for you, hasn't it?'

'Yeah, well,' I replied. 'It was pretty awesome.' I knew he wasn't really interested, so I asked what he had planned for tomorrow.

'Nothing much,' he said. 'What about you? What would you like to do?'

'What about the Golden Bridge?' I said. 'I'd like to see it up close.'

So that's what we did. Dickie booked two tickets for a tour of Muir Woods and Sausalito, which took us over the Bridge and into some nice country with huge trees and that. We had lunch in this Sausalito place, which is a kind of fishing village turned marina. Quaint, like, but touristy. The afternoon we spent touring the town itself. It's quite a place is San Francisco, and I wouldn't mind living there meself if it wasn't for the earthquakes they have all the time.

Dickie didn't seem interested in any shopping and went to bed early. Our flight wasn't till the following afternoon, but he seemed to want to get home as quick as possible, as if everything was over, and I was wondering if this really was the end of the line for me or what. Anyway, we got to the airport all right, and flew to LA on time, so we had quite a wait for the London connection. I was getting my usual duty-frees, when he gave me an envelope.

'What's this, Dickie?'

'The pearl I bought in Tahiti,' he replied. 'Take it as a present. A memento, if you like, of this trip.'

I could see the old codger was dead keen to get home, but it looked like another nail in my coffin. I took it with thanks, considering it part of the payoff or golden handshake like. The plane left on time, and we circled smoggy old LA before heading out to sea. I wish they wouldn't do that: you know they're going the wrong way, and you feel you ought to tell them London is East not West. But of course, it turned round eventually, and back we went on course over the North Pole practically. It's a long flight, and we both settled down trying to pass the hours as best we could. I had plenty to think about. What the hell was going to happen to me now, I wondered.

We had a good dinner, and I watched the film before dozing off. When I woke, I was calculating we had another three hours or so to go, when I noticed Dickie wasn't there beside me. He came back after quite a time, and sank into his seat.

'You all right?' I asked.

'Just been sick,' he said. 'Feeling groggy.'

His speech was slurred, and for a moment I wondered if he'd gone back to swig some more champagne, then I noticed he was shaking. 'Terrible headache,' he said. 'Terrible.'

'I'll get some aspirin from the stewardess,' I got to my feet.

'No- aspirin – Steve – need – new brain.'

'Whad'ya mean?' I was getting real frightened. I didn't want to believe what he'd told me before. Surely he wasn't going to die right now.

'I'll get some help,' I said, and rushed to the back of the plane. I told the stewardess what had happened and about the brain tumour and that, and she came forward with me. She said she was a trained nurse, and not to worry, but just stay at the back for a bit. I could see her talking to Dickie in a low voice. It was weird: the low throbbing of the plane pushing its way towards home, and the dark silence of everyone asleep, or trying to sleep. I remembered Eric talking about surreal painting and that, about this guy Dali and surrealism. I was beginning to understand what he was on about.

At last she came back to me. 'He doesn't look too good,' she said. 'I'll get the pilot to radio Heathrow for an ambulance.'

Oh Jesus, no. I can't cope with this. The other stewards were preparing breakfast and switching on the lights. People were pushing back the shades and looking at the dawn coming up ahead. Oh, Jesus, no.

I went back to Dickie lying there. 'How you feeling man?' I asked stupidly. I didn't know what to say, or what to do. Bloody useless I was, when this was when I should be a tower of strength. Business Class wasn't full, so a couple of the stewards helped or half-carried old Dickie to the back, where there were some seats empty. That way he could lie down. This was done so quietly and efficiently that most of the other passengers didn't realise what was going on. Breakfast was served and people were queuing up for the loo to shave and wash and that. I just sat on the seat arm staring uselessly at Dickie; he didn't seem to see me properly. I took his hand, but he didn't react or nothing. Oh, Jesus, I said to myself again. Oh, Jesus.

It never seemed to end, that nightmare – but of course it did. We landed at Heathrow, and an ambulance was waiting. They came on board at once, and carried Dickie off on a stretcher. I followed behind with all our hand baggage. 'What'll I do about our luggage?' I asked. Trying to be efficient.

'Don't worry, sir. We'll keep it for you. You can collect it later.'

I got in the Ambulance and we sped off, the siren shrieking its way through the traffic. Dickie was unconscious, and the paramedics questioned me again about what I knew. 'Brain tumour,' I said. 'That's all I know. Brain tumour. Something called glioma or something.'

They nodded as if they knew, and the ambulance squealed to a halt in front of Hillingdon Hospital. By the time I had collected our hand baggage and that and got out, Dickie had already been whisked into the main building, and I was told to wait for further news. I got myself a coffee and that, and tried to read, but couldn't: just chain-smoked.

After an hour or so, the nurse came to me, and asked if I was a relative.

'Sort of,' I replied, not knowing what to say, but knowing I had to be the one responsible. 'He hasn't got any other close relatives.'

'I'm afraid he's gone into a coma,' she said gravely. 'There's little hope I'm afraid.'

Time takes on a different dimension in moments like these. In the following hours, it ticked ever so slowly, then rushed past so that my memory couldn't take it all in. I was sitting on his bed, looking at that dear old face – sleeping it looked like, not in a coma at all. I took hold of his hand and squeezed it tight. Dear God, I thought, I wish I could do something.

His eyes flickered and opened and he looked out trying to focus like a newborn child. His mouth trembled but he couldn't speak. His eyes finally found me, and he looked at me like he was pleading or something. I didn't know what to do or say. 'How are you, Dickie, me lad?' I said softly, knowing that wasn't the right thing, but what the hell was?

He kept his eyes fixed on mine, and I could feel a slight pressure from his hand. Perhaps he was going to pull through after all.

'D'ya need anything, Dickie, old dear? What can I get ya?'

A trembling smile flickered across his mouth and he stared at me still.

'Dickie,' I said, 'Don't die on me, you silly old bugger. You're my mate. I need you to teach me and that.'

I was close to tears by then, and feeling right helpless. I looked down on that old face, thinking of all the good times we'd had. The best times in my life actually. I took both his hands in mine, and bent down and kissed him on the mouth.

His breath smelt horrible.

His face cleared and I thought a miracle was going to happen. He opened his mouth to say something, but instead it sounded as if he was trying to clear his throat. His eyes closed and his head fell gently to its side on the pillow.

He was gone.

EPILOGUE

Maggie

I felt really sorry for him, the poor wee soul. He came back to Ashford with his tail between his legs – he was really grieving for the man. But it must have been awful having to cope with all that at the airport and hospital, sorting things out. He was quite nice to Alan, thank goodness: I was afraid we'd be having a row or something, but no, he accepted what I'd done, and didn't say much about it. He's still staying in our old flat, and I go round now and then to help him. He's got to sort out the will and Richard's house and effects. He seems to think he's been left something. I asked him what his plans were, but he was a bit vague. But he's got something in mind, that's for sure: he's been looking quite cheerful the last few days. One thing about Steve, he'll live to fight another day, somehow or another.

Alan and I have settled in fine together. Life's not perfect, but then is it ever? He's something of a workaholic: we've opened up his new business, and it's doing fine, but it means Alan's never at home. I help in the shop during the day, but he works all hours, and I'm back alone in front of the telly most evenings, the same as ever. So I'm doing a computer course for beginners so that I'll be able to do the accounts and things and pull my weight in the business. I suppose it'll get better once we're on our feet. At least I hope so.

There is another matter, which might become serious. I'm no getting any younger, and I want kids. Steve pussyfooted round this too, but I've a nasty feeling that Alan doesn't want them at all. His excuse is we're still on the bottom rung, we haven't the money, wait a while. But I haven't got all that while to wait.

Still, the flat's nice, and Alan's a real nice man. It'll all work out in the end, I'm sure.

STEVE

It's a year to the day since Dickie died, so I said a prayer for the old sod. I'm not religious at all, though I got interested in Hinduism and Buddhism and that in India. There must be something, though, else there's not much point in it, is there?

A lot's happened since he died on me in Hillingdon Hospital. It was hard going for a while, I must say, what with having to sort things out and arrange everything. He wanted to be cremated, and so he was at Barham Crematorium one beautiful September morning when the sun shone fit to bust. Your funeral is a great place to see who your friends really are; only problem is you're in no position to view the situation, are you? Unless you're peering down from heaven, like. Dickie's funeral was sad though. I'd put a notice in the local papers as well as his Daily Telegraph, but hardly anyone turned up. His cleaner and her husband, a couple of local shopkeepers (probably in the wine trade), Maggie and Alan and, to my surprise, Janet.

It was nice of them, I thought, turning up to support me, more than Dickie. That's what I meant about friends and that. Poor Janet looked horrible as usual - age isn't doing her any good at all. But Maggie looked great in a black coat and hat with her red hair hanging loose to her shoulders. I made a mess of that relationship and no mistake. But she's turned her loving eyes on Alan, that's clear, so there's not much I can do about it, even if I wanted to. Which I don't. Press on on my own, I suppose.

Dear old Dickie gave me quite a shock with his Last Will and Testament: he left me everything. I expected something, but not the full Monty, so to speak. But when it was all worked out, it turned out to be not as much as I'd thought. The house at St Margaret's wasn't his. At least, it was in a way, but he'd signed it over to this company in return for an annuity to be paid all his lifetime. Meanwhile, he could live in his house until he died. Like having your cake and eating it. Typical Dickie.

But I got the contents, which I sold for quite a nice price. But it was spooky going through his things – not a job anyone likes, that's for sure. I got a shock too when I saw his bedroom; there was a blown up photo of Philip in a silver frame on the chest of drawers, but guess who was smiling at him in glorious Technicolor from the bedside table? He took that one when we were in India, and I was lying by the pool. He had come down from the hotel and I was laying back with me hands behind my head, grinning like a moron.

I knew he was fond of me, but his Will said that I was the son he had never had. Dear old Dickie.

There wasn't much of the readies either. He lived on his annuity and pension and that, but most of the money he got from selling the gems and stuff had been spent on our trips, so he wasn't rich at all. Just seemed so. He'd just wanted one last spree before he died, and I was lucky he chose me to go with him. So when all the house and stuff had been gone through and sorted, and his Will proven and that, I was finally free to get on with my own future.

I'd had quite a long time to work things out, and I reckoned I'd have enough to keep me going for a while, if I didn't blow the lot on high living. Not bad at all, I suppose; but in five years' time I'd be over forty, and then where would I be? There aren't many prospects in digging up roads. I needed a Future, and I had no training for it, so it wasn't going to be easy. I had an idea – a long shot, but it was worth a try. Anything rather than go back to the Job Centre and odd jobs in Ashford.

So after everything was sorted, I put my plan into action. I rang up Nicholas Hoddesdon, the jeweller, in Greville Street, told him about Dickie's death, and made an appointment to see him the following week. He remembered me well, which was an encouraging sign. I got out me books and tried to study all I could about gems, but not much wanted to sink in. I treated meself to a nice conservative suit; black it was, with white shirt and dark blue tie to go with it. And black shoes and socks. I got the sapphire Dickie gave me out of my deposit box, and put the black pearl in its place. Ironic that, 'cos I didn't think much of the pearl like, but loved the sapphire. But I'd keep it as a memento of my time with Dickie, as he had wanted, as long as I could afford to.

So I was all dressed up, fresh-faced and clean-cut when I arrived at Hoddesdon's premises in Greville Street. I had deliberately asked for a 2.30 appointment, because he'd have had lunch by then, and hopefully feeling at peace with the world. Dickie had taught me that one.

He looked quite pleased to see me, and twinkled away as before. We shook hands and got down to business. I showed him my sapphire.

'As you can see, Mr Hoddesdon,' I explained in my best modulated tones, checking my grammar as I went, 'It's quite a remarkable stone.'

He made non-committal noises and got out his loupe to impress me. 'Its qualities can be seen by the naked eye,' I broke in to show him I knew what he was up to. 'Looks like a Kashmir Blue to me.'

'Hmm, possible,' he said.

'As you can see it's been cut cabochon, and is exhibiting asterism.' – I was glad that sentence was out of the way; it had taken a lot of practice – 'It has to be of great value, don't you think?'

He studied it for quite some time, before putting it on the table in front of him. 'How much were you thinking of, Mr Jackman?'

This was the difficult bit. I gave him one of my cheerful grins and said: 'I don't know, Mr Hoddesdon.'

He raised his eyebrows. 'Don't know, Mr Jackman?' he smiled. 'That's a dangerous position to put yourself in, is it not?'

'Possibly,' I replied. 'But I trust you, Mr Hoddesdon.'

'Thank you,' he bowed graciously.

'But I'm not sure I'm selling it, you see,' I went on.

'Oh? Then why are you – ?'

'Mr Hoddesdon,' I said, 'I'm putting myself at your mercy. It's like this. As I told you, Mr Grayson died suddenly while we were away.'

'I was so sorry,' he said automatically.

'Yes, well. I am now unemployed.'

'Oh dear.'

'But one thing Dic – Mr Grayson taught me was a love for gems.'

The eyebrows went up again. 'You love them?'

'Yes, I do.'

'They're not simply a means of acquiring a profit?'

'No, Mr Hoddesdon. Much more than that.' I picked up the sapphire and laid it on the palm of my hand. 'Look at that stone, Mr Hoddesdon. Never mind its price. Just look at it. Doesn't its beauty make you want to weep?'

He looked at me over the top of his glasses. 'You surprise me, Mr Jackman, you really do.'

'Well it's true, Mr Hoddesdon. Mr Grayson taught me a lot, but more than anything, he taught me to look at things in a different light. I love these gems, Mr Hoddesdon, very much indeed.'

Now I took a deep breath. 'And that's why I'm here. I'd really like to work in this business, and learn the trade.'

He raised his hand as if to defend himself from attack. 'No, no Mr Jackman. Quite out of the question. It takes years to acquire the knowledge of...'

'I can wait. I don't expect much. Just the chance to learn and work with you.'

He shook his head, and once he started he couldn't stop. 'No, no, no. I'm sorry to...'

'I know the days of apprenticeship are over, Mr Hoddesdon, and anyway I'm much too old to be put in that category, but I wondered if I could make some sort of payment.'

'Payment?'

'Yes.' I held out my sapphire and put it in his hand. 'This, for instance. If I gave you this sapphire as a token of my good faith, would you accept me as a kind of pupil?'

His mouth opened. ' I've never heard of such a thing. We don't operate like that.'

'Please, Mr Hoddesdon, think about it. I'm sorry Mr Grayson isn't here to give you a reference, but I can tell you I'll always be honest, reliable and straightforward with you. You can trust me.'

'It's not that. I...' He didn't finish. He put down the sapphire like it was red-hot. 'Have you any idea, Mr Jackman, how much this is worth?'

'Yes, I have. Not like you, of course. But I can make a rough guess.'

'Well, then. It would be impossible for me to accept -'

'Look on it as a guarantee, Mr Hoddesdon.'

'Guarantee?'

'Yes. Of my enthusiasm, integrity and real interest. You take the stone, allow me to work here without payment until you consider I am worth paying, and we're both happy. You can't lose, and neither can I.'

'Suppose you're not suitable?'

'Then I've tried and it hasn't worked out. It's not the end of the world, you know. Something else will turn up, but at least I've tried.'

He stared at me for what seemed a lifetime. He had a nice face; kind of nondescript, but nice, with the longest whitest hands I've ever seen. A gem in his hands became enhanced and took on a glow when he was handling them. I reckoned he was a sober uptight closet queen, but I can handle that. He needs a bit of cheering up, and I'm good at that.

At last he spoke: 'You realise you would not be in a position of trust or responsibility for a long, long time – if ever.'

I nodded.

'And I must warn you, the chances of you succeeding are slight.'

I nodded again. He sighed and shook his head. He picked up the sapphire in his white hands and held it lovingly. 'I'll think about it, Mr Jackman. Meanwhile, take it back.' He handed it to me, and got up. He held out his hand, which I took with one of my cheerful grins. I was glad to see the twinkle come back in his eyes

Nevertheless, on the train back home I felt real miserable: I thought I'd blown it. What a useless git I am, I said to myself. Bloody useless. When I called Maggie, she said I was acting like a whore, but I said it was no worse than a woman uncrossing her legs at a job interview. I'd never betray him, or let him down. Look how I'd behaved with Dickie.

So I was right surprised when he rang me a couple of days later to say he would agree to my offer, but repeated all the dire warnings.

So here I am working away under Nickie. First Dickie, now Nickie. He's turned out to be a real nice guy: lonely like Dickie, but passionate about gems. He loves them and imparts this love to me. I'm learning every day. I've earned his trust, and am allowed to handle various stones as they come in.

His old workman, Fred, has been a real good mate to me. I'm now working as an assistant benchman, setting stones into jewellery. Fred's had the patience to teach me when times were slack, and he says I've got a talent for it. Imagine me with a talent! He'll be retiring in a few years' time, so I can live in hopes, can't I? I also welcome customers, and make myself useful. Nickie's already paying me a small salary – 'to avoid slave labour' is the way he puts it; but he obviously thinks I'm worth it. He keeps himself to himself that one, and I don't think there's anybody outside the office either. He did take me to dinner recently to celebrate the fact I was now 'on his staff'. He asked me about Dickie and was curious about our relationship, but I wasn't giving anything away. Dickie's life and loves are safe with me. But Nickie never let slip anything about himself. I know he likes me, but like Dickie, he's a gentleman, and won't make a move out of place. He continues to twinkle when he sees me though.

Yeah, I'm going to make a go of this all right, and no mistake. I'll buy meself a small pad near here and get the hell out of Ashford. Maybe even fall in love, marry and have kids. That'd be nice, but I've a feeling it's not on the cards for me. I think of Rana quite a lot – think of going back and trying again with her. Wouldn't work out though, would it? Funny how you always want the unattainable. Perhaps I think too much of meself to love another person like Dickie did. I dunno. It'd be nice though.

I often think of Dickie on the train going home – think of the times we had together. I suppose he was the best friend I ever had. He knew how to love, and I don't.

I wonder if I ever will.